# "I'm Not Going To Make Love To You Here. Not Now."

"Why not?" Abby asked.

"You need more time to consider what you're giving away," Matt responded.

"I'm more concerned about what I might lose," she murmured. "And I don't mean my virginity."

"What about that husband in the future? He'll know."

"Maybe he'll have to accept me as I am."

As she was. Beautiful. Abby was pure joy to look upon, to be with. She dragged him out of his world of business deals, competition with himself and with others, even out of the pain of the past. He could see need in her eyes, desire, and he wanted more than anything to give her the pleasure she so longed for.

Yet, did he dare take from her the one treasure she'd safeguarded all her life? Abby claimed she was ready. But could he believe her?

Dear Reader,

Welcome to Silhouette Desire, the ultimate treat for Valentine's Day—we promise you will find six passionate, powerful and provocative romances every month! And here's what you can indulge yourself with this February....

The fabulous Peggy Moreland brings you February's MAN OF THE MONTH, *The Way to a Rancher's Heart*. You'll be enticed by this gruff widowed rancher who must let down his guard for the sake of a younger woman.

The exciting Desire miniseries TEXAS CATTLEMAN'S CLUB: LONE STAR JEWELS continues with *World's Most Eligible Texan* by Sara Orwig. A world-weary diplomat finds love—and fatherhood—after making a Plain Jane schoolteacher pregnant with his child.

Kathryn Jensen's *The American Earl* is an office romance featuring the son of a British earl who falls for his American employee. In *Overnight Cinderella* by Katherine Garbera, an ugly-duckling heroine transforms herself into a swan to win the love of an alpha male. Kate Little tells the story of a wealthy bachelor captivated by the woman he was trying to protect his younger brother from in *The Millionaire Takes a Bride*. And Kristi Gold offers *His Sheltering Arms*, in which a macho ex-cop finds love with the woman he protects.

Make this Valentine's Day extra-special by spoiling yourself with all six of these alluring Desire titles!

Enjoy!

*Joan Marlow Golan*

Joan Marlow Golan
Senior Editor, Silhouette Desire

Please address questions and book requests to:
Silhouette Reader Service
U.S.: 3010 Walden Ave., P.O. Box 1325, Buffalo, NY 14269
Canadian: P.O. Box 609, Fort Erie, Ont. L2A 5X3

# The American Earl
## KATHRYN JENSEN

Published by Silhouette Books

**America's Publisher of Contemporary Romance**

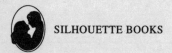 **SILHOUETTE BOOKS**

ISBN 0-373-76347-6

THE AMERICAN EARL

Copyright © 2001 by Kathryn Pearce

Visit Silhouette at www.eHarlequin.com

**Printed in U.S.A.**

## KATHRYN JENSEN

has written many novels for young readers as well as for adults. She speed walks, works out with weights and enjoys ballroom dancing for exercise, stress reduction and pleasure. Her children are now grown. She lives in Maryland with her writing companion—Sunny, a lovable terrier-mix adopted from a shelter.

Having worked as a hospital switchboard operator, department-store sales associate, bank clerk and elementary school teacher, she now splits her days between writing her own books and teaching fiction writing at two local colleges and through a correspondence course. She enjoys helping new writers get a start, and speaks "at the drop of a hat" at writers' conferences, libraries and schools across the country.

To Linda Hayes, of Columbia Literary Associates,
a superlative agent and even more valued friend.
May your retirement bring you exciting new adventures
and rich satisfaction. Thank you for everything... KJ

# One

Matthew Smythe marched into the empty room, his executive assistant trailing in his irate wake like a tiny skiff bobbing helplessly behind a battleship. "Why isn't this room ready?" he snapped. "*Where* is Belinda?"

Paula Shapiro gave a weary sigh. "Sir, she quit this morning. Remember?" Like most men, including her own nearly grown sons, the young president of Smythe International only listened to what he wanted to hear.

"That's ridiculous! The woman only took the job two months ago."

"I suppose, like the others, she found the work—" Paula searched for a safe word "—demanding. It isn't easy arranging these things on the spur-of-the-moment." *Or coping with your temperament,* she added silently.

"A tasteful reception for a few clients. How difficult can that be?" he grumbled. Matt's sharp eyes quickly scanned the bare room. A bar should have been set up, along with a table of imported delicacies in front of the expanse of bronzed glass overlooking a breathtaking Chicago skyline. Comfortable seating ought to have replaced the metal folding chairs.

Vaguely, he recalled that his latest in a long line of social secretaries had sounded upset about something earlier that day. But her feminine hysterics had barely made a dent in his busy mind. Perhaps he should have paid better attention. Paula had been out of the office on an errand for him or she would have been aware of the pending emergency. But it was too late now.

He glared at his watch. Less than two hours and his guests would arrive. He raked fingers through thick, dark hair. "What do you suggest we do?"

"I could call your caterer," Paula suggested doubtfully. "But that won't sell your products for you."

Matt shook his head. "And tomorrow around noon, Franco would show up with a smashing spread. No, do it yourself. We have everything you'll need."

"Lord Smythe!" Paula's chin dropped a full two inches, eyes narrowing to slits, fists settling on matronly hips.

Not a good sign, Matt thought. An intelligent, middle-aged woman, Paula sported a froth of blond, permed hair and spectacles with glittering thingies at the pointed corners. She also efficiently managed his office and accepted long hours of work without complaint, for which he paid her generously. But when she used his aristocratic title and that chin fell, he knew he'd gone too far.

"I reminded you just five minutes ago." Her glare intensified. "I have to take my youngest to a dental appointment today."

"Oh…well, of course. Sorry. Do you have any other ideas for this reception?" He could set out the food himself, but he wasn't sure that he'd do a very good job of it. And it still left him in the lurch for a hostess, which had been the other part of Belinda's job.

"If you're really in a jam," a mellow female voice spoke up from the doorway, "I could bring in a few gourmet items I think you'd be pleased with."

Matt swung around to see a petite young woman standing at the entrance to the conference room. The first thing he noticed was her tumble of red hair. It must have been windy outside, because tendrils had been whisked every which way, yet still gleamed and managed to look terribly becoming as a frame around her elfin features. Her second remarkable feature were her long legs. If she'd been wearing anything less conservative than the navy blue suit, its skirt cut demurely below the knee, she would have been inviting trouble just by stepping outside her home. He studied her further. With the flaming hair, he expected her eyes to be green. They were not. They suggested rich mocha tones and glittered at him enthusiastically. He felt an immediate hot tug from within his body.

*"Who* are *you?"* he grumbled.

She produced a business card as swiftly as Annie Oakley drawing her six-shooter. Stepping forward, she thrust the little pink rectangle into his fingers. "Abigail Benton," she announced in a crisp voice. "I represent the Cup and Saucer, a coffee-and-pastry shop here in Chicago. Perhaps you've heard of us?"

She didn't wait for an answer. Words bubbled from her pretty lips etched in a luscious berry-rich shade of gloss. "I'm in the building for a meeting, but I'm running early. If you like, I could collect the necessary supplies and set up the room for you. How many are you entertaining tonight?"

He viewed her speculatively. The raised color in her cheeks and the way she pushed herself halfway up onto her toes as she spoke made him suspect she wasn't as confident as she was pretending to be. Nevertheless, the woman was putting on a damned fine show. And, admittedly, he was in a sticky situation. Anything she could do for him would be better than nothing.

"Three couples and myself," he said, turning to leave the room. "Paula, show her where everything is then get that young man's teeth fixed."

Back in his private office, Matt pulled his guests' files in front of him, covering the family crest embossed in gold on the black leather of his desk blotter. He began to review the personal as well as professional profiles in each folder. After only a few minutes, he pushed them away in frustration, unable to concentrate. All he could see was that damned explosion of crimson hair…and her eyes. Abigail Benton's eyes had been remarkable.

Ruthlessly, he forced his thoughts back to the matter at hand.

Although immediate disaster had been averted, he wondered what the devil he was going to do about the rest of this week's meetings. And next week's? His schedule was packed. He *needed* a full-time hostess and social secretary. Smythe International was known for entertaining its business associates in style.

Glamorously intimate dinner parties for his foreign exporters. Cozy receptions for American retailers whose upscale shops he supplied. Lavish entertainment had paid off for Matthew Smythe, seventh earl of Brighton. His catalog carried hundreds of delicious items from all over the world—famed Valrona chocolates made in France, Neapolitan coffees, Turkish spices and dainty British biscuits to nibble with a cup of bergamot-scented Earl Grey tea on a lazy afternoon.

But he needed a reliable staff to pull it all off. Tomorrow he would begin interviewing for Belinda's replacement. But until then...

He glanced down at the business card tossed absently on his desk. Abigail, an old-fashioned name despite her wild beauty. She was young and, if he had accurately read her body language, inexperienced in her trade. Perhaps inexperienced on many levels. There had been that telltale layer of nervousness beneath her bright-eyed enthusiasm. He was probably a fool for trusting a stranger to such an important task. But it was either let her do whatever she could, or ship his entire party off to a restaurant. That would do neither his sales pitch nor his reputation any good. And so, he'd just have to take the risk.

Abby stood in the center of an immense temperature-controlled vault, looking around with all the prickly excitement of a child left unattended in a candy shop. She had been working for the Cup and Saucer for nine months. It beat selling perfume at a department store or waiting on tables at Burger Delite, both of which she'd done while in college and grad school at Northwestern.

Hopefully, those days were behind her. She was a salaried employee now. Minimum wage, true, but with a commission! And she loved her job.

Two days before her twenty-fifth birthday, she had finished graduate work for her master's degree in retail marketing. The trick then had been to find a job, and she figured she might as well choose one she enjoyed. While still a student, she had loved treating herself to a cappuccino or herb tea at the Cup and Saucer—when she could afford the luxury. But even when cash was hard to come by, she had adored browsing through the rainbow of exotic teas and coffees, the imported sweets, delicate pastries, home-made cranberry-orange muffins and Chunk o' Chocolate cookies. This was a world in which she'd be content to give up her last breath.

The last time she'd gone home to the little farm south of Alton, Illinois, she had confided her dreams to her mother. "I'll work for a few years, saving my money, learning everything I need to know about the gourmet food industry," she explained. "When the time is right, I'll finance the rest and open my own little shop. Down on the Navy Pier between the arcade and that cute little jewelry store—that would be perfect." She tingled with excitement.

"How nice, dear," her mother had said with a patient smile and a pat on her daughter's arm. She might as well have added, *It's good for a girl to have a hobby until she starts her family.* Clearly, confiding in her mother was a wasted effort.

Actually, a family was only part of Abby's dream. She wanted a husband and babies, of course, but first she wanted to prove to herself that she could be really good at doing something other than making babies.

With a sigh, Abby began selecting jars of imported calamara and Spanish black olives, fresh fruits, wax-sealed wedges of Stilton and Brie cheese, colorfully wrapped packets of crackers and tins of cookies from the shelves around her. She would aim for a balance of sweet and salty, pungently spiced and delightfully mild foods—since she didn't know the tastes of the guests. Setting her loot aside on a long shelf, she opened the massive door of a walk-in freezer. Inside was a wheeled cart and, along the walls, packaged rolls, pastries, breads and meats.

Abby loaded up the cart, feeling intoxicated with shopping power. Where had the man bought all of this yummy stuff? She took mental notes of brands and country origins. Whoever the guy was, he had great taste and a genius for a supplier. Maybe he too bought from Smythe Imports, since they were in the same building. Actually on the same floor. She couldn't find a name plaque anywhere to identify the owner of the conference room.

Glancing at her watch, she gasped. She'd been thirty minutes early for her appointment. If she hurried she could still make it without being too late.

By the time forty minutes had flown by, Abby finally finished setting up. The conference room looked inviting and cozy, the way she'd want a room to feel if she'd been traveling and longed for soothing surroundings. The bar included both chilled spring water and hot water for herb teas, along with a variety of wines and ingredients for cocktails. A round buffet table displayed a combination of imported and domestic delicacies.

She was sorely tempted to nibble, as hungry as she was. But there wasn't even time to hunt down anyone and tell them she was done. Abby dashed breathlessly down the hall, reading off numbers on office doors as she flew past. She was ten minutes late for her meeting but, with any luck, the sales rep would be running late, too. Ordinarily the reps came to the Cup and Saucer, but she had wanted an excuse to see the offices of the prestigious importer.

She found the suite of rooms marked Smythe International and threw her body through the door—only to run into a wall of muscle and suit that let out a deep, "Ooomph."

"Oh, sorry, I just…" But her apology was cut short as she ricocheted off the barrier and into the doorframe. Two strong hands viced her shoulders, bringing her back onto her feet and holding her upright until she stabilized.

Slowly Abby looked up at the strikingly handsome man she'd met earlier. She frowned, puzzled. "I'm so sorry," she managed between gasps. "I guess I was in…in too much of a hurry."

He glared darkly at her. "What's the problem?"

"There's no problem at all. I've finished setting up your room."

He scowled critically at her hair, then his eyes slid down over her department-store suit in a way that made her feel self-conscious. "You'll need to change."

"Pardon me?"

"That sort of conservative getup hardly does justice to epicurean foods and fine wines."

She stared up at him, for the first time aware of just how tall he was in comparison to her petite five-foot-three-inch figure. A good four inches over the six-foot mark, she'd guess. Built like Gibraltar. And there was something strangely familiar about him, although she doubted she'd ever met him before. "I think there's been a slight misunderstanding here." She tried out a diplomatic smile on him, but it seemed to have no effect. "You see, I have an important meeting. I'm late as it is. I only offered to help because you seemed to be in a bind."

"Out of the goodness of your heart, right?" His tone was flat with sarcasm.

Abby stiffened, her smile gone. "That's right. Some people are just plain nice. Now I'm overdue for my appointment with the sales rep for Smythe International. So if you'll excuse me." She tried to slip past him, but he stepped smoothly into her path.

"I sent Brian home for the day."

She frowned. The words didn't make sense to her. But the way he was looking at her made it impossible for her to untangle them. She could feel his gaze peeling away layers. Of clothing, certainly, but also reaching beneath, as if he were analyzing her for a particular purpose. Abby didn't like the feeling. But she wasn't going to let him rattle her anymore than he already had. There were more important matters at hand.

"He can't have left!" she objected. "I set up the appointment two weeks ago."

It was as if the man hadn't heard a word. "Where do you live?"

He was incredible! First he mentally disrobed her. Then he expected her to divulge her home address. "I'm sorry, I don't think that's any of your business."

"Oh, bloody hell! I'm not some kind of *masher*." The old-fashioned word sounded comical, following on his cursing. And had she imagined a faint foreign

accent? British? "I just want to know if you have
time to go home and change before the reception. If
not, I think Belinda left a few dresses here." His eyes
did their disturbing trick again. "You look to be similar sizes."

Abby glared at him. "The only place I'm going,
since I've apparently missed my meeting, is back to
work."

"Ah, yes." His eyes lifted and so did the corners
of his lips. "That little coffee shop over on Oak. I've
stopped by a few times." He nodded, keeping his
opinion to himself.

"I'm sorry I can't stay and play hostess for you.
But I'm sure you'll make out fine."

His expression conveyed that he knew she didn't
have a clue how he'd make out. But he wasn't going
to argue the point. "Call your boss and ask for the
rest of the day off. I'll pay you five bills to smile and
make nice to my guests."

Her mouth dropped open. "Five *hundred* dollars?"
A heartbeat later, the implication of the rest of his
sentence struck her. "That isn't the kind of work I
do, Mr. —"

"Matthew Smythe." He held out a hand for her to
shake and at the moment she remembered where
she'd seen him before…or at least his photos. The
last time had been on the cover of *Fortune* magazine.
She immediately seized his hand as if she'd been ordered to. Then, gradually, the implication of all she'd
said up to that moment sank in. She had probably
sounded like a madwoman.

"You're the president of Smythe International,"
she murmured weakly. "The third largest import
company of its kind in this country." She had read

about him in the *Wall Street Journal* and *Fortune,* as well as the society columns in the *Tribune.* He was always referred to as The American Earl—Lord Matthew Smythe—a member of the British aristocracy who had come to America and made himself a second fortune.

"We've done well," he murmured dismissively. "Look, I don't want you to take this the wrong way, Miss Benton. You have to understand, I'm in a rare fix here. An hour from now, three buyers for prosperous, upscale retail companies, along with their wives and traveling companions, will arrive at this suite." He shoved strong fingers through his neatly clipped hair. It fell immediately back into place, every hair in line. "Serving samples of the products I bring into this country doesn't make a strong enough impact to guarantee a sale. I need a partner circling the room, listening for comments, keeping spouses entertained, putting on a gracious face. *I need you.*" The last three words were very nearly a growl.

"But I don't—" She was about to protest that she knew nothing about entertaining elite company when the possible benefits of her situation slammed up against her innate shyness. Five hundred dollars and goodwill toward man aside, the experience and contacts gained from such an evening would be invaluable. She'd be a fool to say no! "I'll change and be back in less than an hour."

"That dress looks good, too. I don't know why you're fussing so much over one little cocktail party." Abby's roommate, Dee D'Angello, sat in the center of Abby's bed, watching her try on the sixth dress in fifteen minutes.

"If you saw in person what *he* looks like, you'd understand," Abby said dryly. "The man is gorgeous. And his suit! Better than an Armani. Had to be hand-tailored." She tugged another dress down over her head and stood before the mirror on her closet door, smoothing out wrinkles. "Do you have any idea of the cost of a tailored suit these days? I'll bet his tie alone cost more than my take-home pay for a week."

"Sounds like someone is hung up on yon company prez," Dee mused.

"Don't be ridiculous. I'm just trying to survive this night so I can pick up some pointers. Smythe is at the top of the heap I want to be in."

"You think by spending one evening in the same room with the man, some of his brilliance will rub off on you?"

Abby laughed, shaking her head. "I'm not that naïve. This is a chance to peek inside the real world of the import-export business. Hanging out with Lord Smythe and his high-powered clients for a couple of hours is more valuable than a year of graduate seminars, better than five years standing behind the counter at a place like the Cup and Saucer. This is how the rich and famous do business!"

"All well and good," Dee admitted, "but be careful. The wealthy live fast lives. People who have more money than they know what to do with use it to get into trouble."

Abby wriggled her toes into a pair of beige slingbacks and studied the effect. "What are you saying?" she asked absently.

"Don't commit yourself to more than you can afford to give." Dee gave her a knowing look from beneath dark, lowered eyelashes.

Abby laughed. "You mean I shouldn't jump into bed with one of Smythe's clients just to cement a deal for him? Don't worry, I won't."

"What about Smythe himself? The man sounds pretty yummy."

Abby considered this new and admittedly interesting possibility then sighed. "He may be great to look at, but the earl has an ego the size of Mount Rushmore and a pompous attitude that would put the British monarchy to shame. No way would I ever consider getting involved with him."

"Right," Dee muttered, plucking a turquoise silk sheath from the bed. "Go with this one."

"Are you sure?" More to the point, was *she* sure? Did she really want to step out of her safe, simple world to sip cocktails and swap market savvy with people whose incomes were ten…maybe a hundred times hers?

Then she remembered Smythe's powerful presence, the way he'd physically blocked her retreat from the reception room until she'd agreed to return. He might as well have handcuffed her to the furniture! Oddly enough, his aggressiveness had excited her at the time. Now, she wondered if it was wise to let a few pleasant chills overwhelm good judgment.

There was still time to back out. She didn't owe the man a thing, she told herself. She could simply retreat into the safe niche she'd carved for herself at the little neighborhood shop two blocks from the campus.

But something beckoned to her from the fifteenth-floor suite overlooking exclusive Lake Shore Drive and the steely waters of Lake Michigan. She knew in the space of one breath that she would go to him.

\* \* \*

She wasn't coming. Matthew could feel it in his bones. She had promised, but the nervous little mouse had succumbed to cold feet. He should have offered her more money, Matthew thought as he paced the carpeted hallway and, on every pass, glared at the polished brass elevator doors. He had already welcomed two of his guests and their companions, and ushered them into the reception room.

The elevator dinged; doors slid open. He looked up out of his black mood, a tight smile ready for his remaining guests. Prepared to take a firm forward step to greet them, he faltered at the vision before him.

Abigail had worn no wrap, the night being warm. Her shoulders, lightly freckled with burgundy-wine specks, were bare and as creamy as fresh milk. The dress was strapless, clinging to her as if by sheer willpower. It molded her body, yet didn't seem slinky or cheap. Its lines were too simple to be couturier; the garment might have been home-sewn. But the exquisite shade of turquoise complimented beautifully the waves of rusty-red hair that spilled over her shoulders and curved round her delicate chin. He liked everything he saw. And everything he imagined hidden by everything he saw.

She stepped off the elevator and looked up at him with a raised brow as if to say, *Big deal, so I'm here.*

"You're late," he said gruffly. "Four of my guests are already inside."

"Then what are you doing out here?"

*Waiting for you!* he nearly snapped, but held back. He didn't want her thinking he doubted she would show. Stepping around to her side, he lifted her hand

and slipped it through the crook in his arm. She tensed.

"Relax," he said, "this is for the sake of appearances."

"Appearances?" She slanted him a look drenched with suspicion.

"It's easier for me if my guests assume my hostess is also..." *My lover.* Why had those words popped into his head when others less suggestive would have done just as well? "That we're—"

"A couple?" she supplied demurely.

"Exactly. I like to be free to talk business without feeling obligated to flirt."

"This is a major problem for you?" She flashed him a wicked little grin. "Fending off smitten clients or their girlfriends?"

Coming from her and said in that way, it did sound ridiculous. But yes, occasionally, the overtly sensual way in which women reacted to him had put him in some tight spots. Business was business. Sex had its own time and place in his life but, so far as he was concerned, the two had never been meant to mix.

"If you're going to be a smartass," he growled, "I don't want you here."

She straightened up and dug in her heels, bringing them both to an instant halt. "*You* were the one who brought up the subject, Lord Smythe. I have to know something about you if I'm to pretend to be your girlfriend." Her eyes flashed in challenge at him before softening again. "Did you mean it—about the five hundred dollars?"

"Of course."

She nodded, satisfied.

It didn't hurt his feelings that playing his girlfriend

seemed so unpleasant a task to her it required substantial compensation. *Never liked redheads anyway,*
he told himself. Although none he'd ever met had
been as stunning as this one.

He shoved that thought immediately aside. Down
to business...

"There are a few things you need to know before
we go in there." He took a breath and focused on her
face, turned up solemnly to meet his. "The rather
portly gentleman is Ronald Franklin of—"

"Of Franklin & James, the shops in every mall
across this country?" she gasped.

"The same. He and his wife don't like to be
pushed. Not a word to him about products, purchases
or marketing strategies. Just keep them company and
let them choose what they want to eat and drink. They
have a new grandchild, you might want to hit on that
angle."

She nodded and shot him a fleeting look that
seemed slightly disapproving, but he couldn't be sure
what she might have found fault with. "And the other
couple?"

"Ted Ramsey and his date."

She didn't need to say a word. He could tell by the
way her eyes lit up that she already knew. She was
good. Very good.

"The casino mogul," Abby murmured after a moment.

"Mogul?" He tipped his head to one side, considering the title, which seemed rather exalted for a real-
estate speculator who had started out as a Brooklyn
landlord and now built flashy gambling palaces in Ve-
gas and Atlantic City. In Matt's view, the man had
thrown a lot of money around and just been lucky.

That kind of fast, sloppy luck didn't often last. "Call him what you will, he's considering introducing upscale import shops into his casinos, and the projected volume of sales is hefty. I'd like to be the one to supply him."

"Understandably. How do I approach him?"

"You don't, unless you can't help it. Be polite, but no sexy little smiles or we could lose the sale. The woman with him is new. He's crazy about her but, word has it, she's the jealous type. Play up to her. Make her feel like a queen, and avoid eye contact with him."

She let out a little puff of air and shook her head. "How do you find out all this stuff? Employ moonlighting CIA agents to spy for you?"

"Nothing so dramatic." He didn't intend to explain the way he worked to her. "Come on, let's go." He gave her arm a tug. "The Duprés should arrive soon; she owns a chain of gift shops throughout New England."

This time, she let him guide her through the door. The two couples turned toward them, and Matt made the introductions. Abby smoothly peeled the grandparents away after a few minutes and guided them toward the buffet table. He noticed she helped herself to a generous plateful of food, then realized she probably hadn't had time to eat before returning to the building. Normally he frowned on his employees chowing down in front of guests, but he noticed that the Franklins seemed to take her cue and also served themselves more than a token taste of each item on the table. Perhaps a good sign.

His attention returned to Ramsey and his companion. The man was a short, rude bully. Matt didn't like his manner or the way he did business, but that was beside the point. He still wanted him as a client, and Ramsey must have sensed it. He started talking money right away while his blond princess stood wide-eyed at the figures being tossed back and forth.

Twenty minutes later, the Duprés arrived. Matt didn't want to leave Ramsey since he sensed they were closing in on a deal, but he couldn't ignore his new arrivals. At a signal from him, Abby gracefully excused herself from the Franklins and made her way across the room to greet the newcomers. Minutes later, she'd brought all four of her guests together around the bar and the two women were laughing at something Abby had said. The men were observing her with discreet admiration. Matt was impressed.

He wrapped up his discussion with Ramsey, who excused himself to leave for another appointment. The gleam in the man's beady, black eyes as he sought out his voluptuous date left Matt with the impression that the setting for the upcoming meeting would more likely include a bed than a desk.

Matt came up behind Abby and rested his hand on her waist. To her credit, she didn't jump. She turned with a ready smile and looked up at him. "I'm having such a lovely chat with our guests. Did you know Caroline does watercolors? She's quite an accomplished artist."

"Oh, no," Mrs. Franklin objected, beaming nevertheless. "I'm a rank amateur."

Matt smiled vaguely…then grunted in pain. Was that an elbow jabbing him in the ribs? "Love to see your work," he blurted out, then glanced down at Abby to make sure he'd gotten the right message.

She looked pleased.

"Oh, I'd be so flattered," the woman cooed. "Do you make it out to the West Coast very often?"

"I have a house in Los Angeles," he said.

"And a penthouse apartment in New York, I hear," her husband put in with a wink. "As well as property in Bermuda. The earl likes a variety of settings."

Matt nodded. "I also enjoy offering my business colleagues a choice of locations for our meetings. You should all join me in Bermuda for a week this September. It's a beautiful time of year there; most of the tourists have gone." There was also the estate in England, given to him by his father. But he hadn't returned to the country of his birth since his twenty-first birthday.

Mrs. Franklin smiled hopefully at Abby. "Oh, and would we see you there, my dear? Ronald hates shopping, but I so love it when I have company."

Abby hesitated, looking unsure of what to say.

"I'm trying to convince her," Matt said quickly, "to spare the time from her busy schedule." He gave Abby's hand a hard squeeze. "Right, darling?"

She grinned weakly. "He can be very persuasive."

By eleven o'clock the remaining guests were taking their leave. Matt called for his driver to deliver the two couples to their hotels. When he came back from seeing them off at the elevator, he found Abby wrapping up leftovers and clearing the buffet table.

"Don't bother with that," he said.

"It will spoil if it's not put away," she objected.

"The cleaning crew will trash it when they come through in a few hours."

"You'd *waste* all of this?" Her eyes were huge at

the suggestion. "There must be hundreds of dollars worth of fantastic stuff here."

"Take it with you if you like."

"Really?"

Her reaction was charming—as open and guileless as a child's in her amazement at the unexpected gift of free eats. Yet he'd seen her in action that night, and she had been mature, intelligent and even a little crafty in the way she had handled his guests. He hadn't heard her pitch one of his products, yet he felt sure his marketing director would receive calls for orders the next day.

He stepped closer to her, watching as she pulled a paper bag out from beneath the table and started packing rewrapped portions of meats, cheeses and pastries into it.

"Thanks, this is really nice of you," she murmured as she worked quickly. "My roommate and I will eat for a week off of this."

"Really," he said, moving still closer. He liked the way she smelled. Not highly cologned, still fresh from her hurried washup hours before.

He wagered she was a woman who favored long, sudsy baths. An enticing thought. A sudden image of her long legs intertwined with his beneath a cloud of bubbles sent a spur of heat into his lower regions. He stepped away from her hastily, forcing his mind back to unfinished business. Taking out his money clip he peeled off five crisp hundred-dollar bills.

When she turned with her bag of food clutched to her chest, her glance dropped to his hand. "Oh, you really don't have to—"

"Take it." She obviously could use the money.

What was she getting for her little sales job? Not much more than minimum wage, he'd venture.

"But I had a really nice time. I don't think I really earned all that money, Lord Smythe."

"Matt," he heard himself say.

She frowned at him. "All right. Matt. I'm sure I got as much out of tonight as you did. I enjoyed meeting your guests…and this is enough of a bonus." She held up her bagged goodies.

*"Take the bloody money,"* he repeated, his voice a notch lower.

She looked warily up into his eyes, like a small animal gauging the next move of a predator. "All righty," she said and slowly reached out to pluck the bills from his hand.

Their fingertips touched, grazed, and his noticeably warmed. The sensation only lasted for an instant, but he was sure it wasn't his imagination. He thought he saw her lips tremble. She took a step backward. His glance settled on her bare shoulders. He ached to brush his lips along them.

"I'd better be going now," she whispered.

"Do you have a car?"

"I'll call a cab."

"My driver will be back soon. We'll drop you off at your place."

He sensed that she was about to object to this too, but something made her think better of it. Abby's gently parted lips closed along a smooth line, and she nodded in acquiescence.

She was certainly the most intriguing woman he'd met in a very long time.

# Two

The limousine wasn't one of those silly stretch jobs the length of a bowling alley that teenagers chip in to hire for their proms. Lord Matthew Smythe's car was all business. It seated only six passengers behind the driver's privacy screen and was furnished with the essential tools of any corporate president—a cell phone, laptop computer with modem and faxing capability, and miniature television to catch late-breaking financial and political news. The CD player and modest wet bar were his only concessions to entertainment. He admitted they had come in handy when his sole guest happened to be an attractive woman in the mood to relax…with him.

The vehicle was black inside and out—a leather-lined cave that glided through the city or down an endless highway smoothly, silently. He liked it better than any of his houses, for it was simple, efficient, mobile and beautiful. Here, he could think and work without distractions, or just remove himself from the world.

Abby sat as far as possible to one end of the half-moon bench seat, staring out the window with determination. She looked very young and equally vulnerable. He sensed she was at least a little afraid of him—although why he had no idea. He tried not to pay too much attention to her long legs.

"You were very good tonight," he murmured after they had driven awhile.

A timid smile twitched the corner of her lips. But she didn't face him, yet. "Thank you."

"I need a full-time hostess."

Now she did turn. Her coffee-and-cream eyes were richer, darker in the dim interior of the car. "Are you offering me a job?"

"Yes." His instincts where people were concerned were always on target. He *knew* she'd be good.

She looked more thoughtful than surprised. "What does the position entail?"

"Just what you did tonight. Orchestrate my guests' entertainment and be on hand to greet them with me."

She tilted her head to observe him critically. "That's hardly full-time work."

"You'll be expected to travel with me to my other locations of business."

"You have offices as well as houses in L.A., New York and Bermuda?" she asked.

"The villa on Bermuda isn't really an office— though I've probably closed as many deals there as anywhere. My Japanese and German exporters particularly like it."

Something unsettlingly perceptive twinkled from

behind her lovely eyes. "And you expect me to quit my job and fly off with you to party—is that it?"

He tensed, ready to vehemently deny her assessment of his lifestyle. He didn't *party* for a living; he had worked damn hard to get where he was. But he refused to let a glorified shop girl drag him into a debate over his business tactics.

"I expect a clever young woman like yourself," he said slowly, "will choose the better of the two jobs." If that didn't satisfy her, she wasn't as smart as he thought she might be.

She gave him a long look. Yes, he mused, the wheels behind those amazing eyes were turning fast and furiously.

"I gather from the little Paula told me, your hostesses don't last very long."

"They obviously haven't been right for the job," he countered.

"But I am?"

"I think so."

She nodded, keeping her thoughts to herself. Matt had never liked being kept waiting. She made him feel painfully restless. He was tempted to shake an answer out of her, but restrained himself.

"And how do I know I won't find myself out of work in a few weeks?" she asked at last.

"Think, Abby. What the bloody hell are you going to learn serving up cappuccinos to college students? I'm offering you a chance to connect with people who run some of the most prosperous and prestigious companies in the world."

"I know that!" she snapped, her eyes flashing. "I just need to understand where I stand. And I would want a contract...for a year."

"You have it," he said.

She blinked, looking surprised that she'd immediately received what she had asked for. "And my duties will be limited and spelled out in it." Although she sounded prim and proper, she failed to look the part with her long, silky legs angled across the limo's black leather cushions.

"Your responsibilities will be catalogued in detail," he agreed. He wasn't going to give her the satisfaction of acknowledging the unofficial tasks she was so nervous about. He'd never played around with any of his employees.

But he couldn't help it if his thoughts wandered delightfully in that direction now. Abby smelled wonderful. And that particular shade of red in her hair made him think twice about bothering with blondes and brunettes ever again. She was luminous.

"Because I am *not* going to sleep with you, Mr. Smythe."

Well, there it is, he thought. Now he was going to have to pretend that he actually *cared* about her concerns. "I'm not interested in sleeping with you, Ms. Benton. I would never consider asking any woman for sexual favors in return for employment in my company," he said carefully. The one thing any executive didn't need these days was a sexual harassment lawsuit.

She nodded, apparently satisfied. Whether or not she fully believed him, he couldn't tell. Whether or not he believed himself, he wasn't sure either. Sleeping with Abigail Benton was becoming an increasingly interesting fantasy. The more she tiptoed around the subject, the more he thought about it.

"What will my salary be?" she asked.

He stopped himself from grinning in triumph. She was ready to talk business. How he *loved* winning a battle of wits with a worthy opponent. Selecting a pen and slip of paper from the caddy beside the cell phone, Matt wrote a figure.

She delicately plucked the paper from his hand but scrunched up her nose at it. "Do I have to cover my own travel expenses out of *this?*"

"Of course not."

She sighed. "My wardrobe is quite limited. I don't know if I can afford to dress the way you would want me to."

*Oh bother,* he thought. He scribbled a higher figure on a second piece of paper, including a generous clothing allowance. She took this one, too.

Her eyes widened, but she sighed again. "I'm sorry. This is more than generous. But, to be honest, it's not a matter of money. I just don't feel this will be a secure position for me. More than anything, that's what I need now." She looked entreatingly across the car at him. "I want to save up and open my own little gourmet shop down by the lake. And I've never intended to leave Chicago, you see. It's my hometown. I really apprecia—"

He violently dashed off a third amount, twice his original offer. The money was of little consequence to him, but he knew the figure would seem outrageously high to her. Thrusting the paper at her, he leaned back and watched with boyish anticipation as her expression changed from frustration to shock.

"Lord Smythe!"

"Matt."

She sighed, her eyes softly appealing, as if she

hoped he would understand her reticence without demanding further explanation.

"Bloody hell," he muttered. He understood all right. She wanted success without risk. And even then, she was scared she might get what she wished for. *Abigail,* he thought, *you need a healthy shove off your safe little lily pad.* And he needed someone like her to continue bringing business his way. Competitors like Joseph Cooper Imports had been breathing down his neck for years. Whatever he had to do to hold them at bay, he'd do.

He wrote one final figure on a fourth scrap. "Last offer," he said tightly. "Don't answer me now. Sleep on it."

She started to speak, but he placed a finger over her lips, silencing them.

"Discuss the offer with your roommate, your parents, your priest—I don't care who. Call me tomorrow with your answer. If you really want to own your own store, or even a chain of stores someday, you'll take a chance with me." She was staring incredulously at the number he'd written. "Look at it this way, the worst that can happen is, I'll work you harder than you've ever worked before. But you'll have your start-up cash four times faster under my employ than with anyone else. And you'll know the business inside out."

The car stopped. The driver came around to open the door. Abby clambered out, a fistful of paper scraps clutched in one hand, her purse and sack of leftovers in the other. She was staring at him in puzzlement, as if hoping, in these last few seconds, she'd discover the ruse he was playing on her.

"No hidden agendas, Ms. Benton. I need smart,

dedicated people around me, and I think you're one of that breed.'' He looked at her sharply, making sure she understood he was serious. "Call me. It's your future.''

Matt flipped a hand at the driver, who closed the door between them. A smile crept outward along his lips. Well, he'd been mostly honest with her. Still, it was a tempting concept—their sleeping together. Very tempting.

As the limo started moving again, he let the thought go. Just let it drift free, like a kite after the string breaks—only he had intentionally cut the cord. If she agreed to work for him, he couldn't afford to turn her into a mistress. She would be too valuable to him in other ways. And, above all, he was a businessman.

Abby slept not at all that night. It wasn't until a thin, rosy dawn broke that she dropped off into an uneasy slumber. She heard the alarm and smacked the snooze button once, twice, then tossed the horrid thing against the wall and collapsed, scrunching her pillow down over her head. She didn't care what time it was, she needed some real sleep.

"So, how'd it go last night?'' a too-chipper voice penetrated the layer of fluff.

Abby tentatively peeked out. It was Dee, bless her cold heart, standing in the bedroom doorway, sipping her morning java from a stoneware mug.

"Leave me alone.''

"It's Saturday. You have to be down at the store by nine, don't you?''

"Oh God, yes. I wasn't even thinking.'' Abby flung the pillow aside and pressed her fingertips to her temples, squinting into the morning light.

"That bad, huh?" Dee guessed. "Boring people, bad food and the boss-man made a pass at you, poor baby."

"Not quite." Abby sat up in bed. "Fascinating people, the best food I've ever eaten and Smythe offered me a job that pays four times what I'm making now."

"Bummer." Dee's eyes twinkled mischievously.

"Knock it off. This isn't funny."

"So, who's laughing? Sounds like you walked into a dream. Why are you looking like a stressed-out ostrich instead of jumping for joy on the bed?"

Abby rolled her eyes, at a loss for words to explain her tangled emotions. "Because I don't trust him. And I don't trust myself to make the right decision."

Dee came and sat on the bed beside her. "Tell Mama."

Abby accepted a sip from her friend's mug then rolled her eyes with the effort of putting her feelings into words. "He's...I don't know...overpowering. You'd have to see him to understand. Matthew Smythe walks into a room, and you just know he's going to waltz out of there with anything he wants. I'll bet he signs deals next week with all three of the bigwigs he was entertaining last night. And when he drove me home in his limo—"

"His li-mo-o-o-o?" Dee arched an ebony brow at her.

"Yes, his limo. When he drove me home after his guests had left, he told me he wanted me to come work for him. When I didn't say yes right away, he kept upping the ante. He swore it was strictly business, no fooling around."

"They all do," Dee mused, but didn't look too unhappy at the thought.

"It sounded as if he *meant* it. That's what bothered me."

"You mean, you *wanted* him to proposition you?"

"Of course not…at least, I don't think I did. But when he didn't I felt kind of…disappointed." Abby agitatedly fluttered her fingers in the air. "It's hard to explain. I just don't trust myself around him. I'm like a spaceship in one of those intergalactic sci-fi flicks. My shields go down."

Dee laughed. "You've really got it bad, girl."

"The irritating thing is, I know the job is absolutely perfect. It would put me miles ahead in my master plan to open my own place. I'd only have to work for Smythe two, maybe three years…and I'd have all my start-up money plus the experience I'd need to run my own business."

"But?"

"But I'd have to keep my shields up."

"And after all this time, you don't really want to, is that it?"

The *all this time* brought a painful twinge of remorse to her heart, for the words didn't refer to the few hours she'd known Lord Matthew Smythe. Dee was referring to the other men who had come into Abby's life, only to be told that she intended to wait for marriage to sleep with anyone. Richad Wooten, the last one, had nearly made it to the altar. *Nearly* being the operative word.

Abby nodded slowly, only now admitting to herself what she'd felt all the night before. "I can't begin to tell you how handsome he is and what he does to my insides.'' She hesitated. "And there's something else.''

"I'm listening.'' Dee sipped her coffee, her eyes never leaving Abby's.

"I'm not sure I believe his promise that it will always be only business between us. And I know that sounds as if I'm contradicting myself—because of what I said about being attracted to him. But I keep asking myself, if he's lying to me about our getting involved, how can I trust him not to lie about other things—like not firing me after just a few months?''

Dee shrugged. "Good point. You'd be working here in Chicago?''

"Some of the time.'' Abby pursed her lips and looked across the bedroom at her collection of tiny crystal animals on the bureau. She'd had some of them since she was in seventh grade, and her parents still added a new one every birthday and Christmas. No matter where she'd lived, even in the dorm at school, they'd been with her. "He travels a lot, keeps offices on the West Coast, in New York, and entertains at his villa in Bermuda.''

"No way.''

"I swear. I'm supposed to accompany him, set up his receptions and parties, play hostess wherever he goes.''

Dee solemnly shook her head. "Definitely a tough life…''

Glaring at her roommate, Abby raised a warning finger. "You're laughing at me.''

Dee winked. "Now would I do that?''

The phone rang before Abby could heave a pillow at her. Reaching across her rumpled sheets, she picked up the receiver.

Before Abby could answer, a voice boomed through the line. "I want your answer now."

"Lord Smythe!" Self-consciously, Abby yanked the sheets up over the front of her thin night-dress...then felt silly when Dee laughed at her knee-jerk gesture of modesty. "I haven't really had a chance to thi—"

"You've slept on my proposal," he stated. "If you don't know your own mind by now, you won't know it any better twenty-four hours from now."

Abby shot a desperate look at Dee, who blinked, looked amused, and was no help at all.

Abby cleared her throat. "Working for you would mean a lot of changes for me. I told you, I've never considered leaving Chicago and—"

"Do you have family here?" he asked.

Was she imagining a gentling of his voice? "Not in the city. But my parents live thirty miles away. I have no brothers or sisters."

"Your parents are in good health?"

"Yes."

"You have a boyfriend?"

"No," she answered automatically, although she would have told any other person interviewing her for a job that such information was none of their business.

"No one serious in your life," he murmured. "And you have no personal commitments. I see."

*What does "I see" mean?* she thought frantically.

"Then tell me, Abby," he asked in a rich baritone that sent curls of warmth through her center, "what is keeping you cemented to this city?"

*What indeed?* she asked herself. Perhaps it was just that she'd never considered living elsewhere. She felt safe here, comfortable within familiar surroundings. Chicago had never seemed a big city to her, even though she'd grown up on a dairy farm. She loved the distinct neighborhoods of the windy city. She had friends in Greektown, shopped the Arab fruit markets and Jewish bakeries and ate in Polish restaurants. She had never considered needing a larger canvas on which to paint her life. Everything she needed to be happy was right here.

Or so she'd always thought.

"Nothing," she whispered into the phone. "Nothing *keeps* me here. It's just my home."

He was silent on the other end, and she could tell this was a silence calculated to let her think about what she'd just said. She did think. She considered the advantages he was offering her…and the dangers. Far more risk was involved in working for Matthew Smythe than she'd ever dreamed of taking. Her stomach felt tied in a knot.

Dee nudged her, hard. When Abby looked up, her friend was mouthing the words—*Take it! Take it! Take it!*

Abby drew a long, deep breath, then let it out very slowly. "I need to give my boss notice."

"I want you to start today."

"But I—"

"Monday morning we'll leave for New York. You'll need the weekend to familiarize yourself with the company's products and the accounts we'll be working on. I'll want you in my office by noon today."

Abby covered the receiver and whispered, "I'm negotiating with Attila the Hun!"

Dee chuckled. ''Honey, aggression's bred into 'em.''

Not into every man, Abby thought. They weren't all as arrogant and bent on having their own way as the entrepreneur aristocrat. Every instinct told her to say *no.* Just to spite the man. But by doing so she would hurt only herself. There were hundreds…thousands of young women who would leap at the chance to work for Smythe, travel the world and be paid far more than they were worth.

Through the line she thought she could hear another voice. A woman's. Abby's ears perked up, but she couldn't make out the exact words.

Then Matt was back on the phone, his tone noticeably gentler. ''If you accept the terms of our agreement and the salary suits you, Paula will be here at the office to brief you. She says just to let her know a convenient time, and she'll make sure she's available.'' He sounded like a schoolboy who'd been taken to task by his teacher. *So there was someone who had found a way to muffle his bark. Interesting,* Abby thought.

''I can't leave my boss at the Cup and Saucer without any help,'' she responded cautiously. ''If I'm able to find someone today to fill in for me until a full-time replacement is hired, I'll come to your office as soon as possible. If not, I'll let you know when I can make it.''

Matt hung up the phone and sat staring at it, considering the conversation he had just had. Abby had never actually said she was taking the job. She simply informed him she would come if and when she could. It was almost as if she was still wrestling with him for control. Control over what, though? He'd always thought that employer–employee relationships were pretty clear-cut. *He* was the one who was supposed to be the boss!

After Paula left the room, he slid lower in the high-backed Scandinavian chair, clunked his heels on the polished teak desktop and thought about all of this before remembering a scene he'd witnessed recently while jogging through Lake Shore Park. He had been running his usual five miles when he spotted a toddler in a bathing suit, standing at the water's edge. She was testing the temperature with the toes of one bare foot, giggling and running back from the lapping wavelets, then touching them again, and again—until she finally worked up the courage to wade in up to her ankles, then her knees, then finally to her waist. At which point she had turned and grinned triumphantly at her parents who were watching with amusement from the shore.

Abby was eager to succeed, and bright, he had no doubt of that, but eternally wary.

Caution was a foreign concept to him. Matt supposed his lack of fear came from never having to worry about failing. His family's money had always provided an excellent safety net. No doubt his brothers felt it, too. When several million sat snugly in a London bank account with your name on it, you didn't worry about making mistakes. What was the worst that could happen? Your latest business venture would flop. Then you'd have to try something different. But you'd bloody well still have a roof over your head and a meal on your plate the next day.

What mattered most to him wasn't making more money. Matt could take or leave that. He supposed the drive to succeed that had spurred him on had more to do with showing his father that he didn't need him, his aristocratic fortune or the estate in the South of England that came with his title. Just as the earl of Suffolk had demonstrated time and again to his sons that he didn't need them. Matt had come to America the first chance he got and made it on his own— *totally* on his own—leaving money, valuable social and business connections, and land behind.

But Abby didn't have scratch.

He knew the type because Paula had been much like her—although somewhat older and with two sons—before she'd come to work for him. Paula used to buy groceries for a month at a time then squirrel them away, making the food last as long as possible. She paid her rent not a day early, keeping it in a savings account to capture those few extra pennies of interest. Nearly all of every paycheck was spent on bills and necessities. Paula had once confided in him that she had maxed out her credit cards months before he hired her.

The idea of Abby ever being able to scrape up enough cash from her old job to start a business was ludicrous.

There were thousands of single people like Paula and Abby—living on the edge but still cherishing their dreams of being out of debt, maybe even owning their own home someday. He didn't think of himself as a philanthropist, but he liked to believe he was giving the men and women he hired a chance to turn their lives around. Some did. Others failed to take advantage of all he was offering them.

Which would it be for Abby?

Matt tossed two files into his briefcase, ordered his

car to be brought around, then returned two important calls. As he strode through the reception area, Paula looked up from her desk.

"Your new gal-Friday called. You were on your line so I took the message. She said she'd be here around two o'clock."

"Good. You'll brief her as we discussed?"

Paula nodded, but gave him a strange look. "You won't be here when she arrives?"

"I have no idea when I'll be back from my appointments. You can do the honors."

He hesitated before stepping into the hallway. "Thank you, Paula, for coming in on a Saturday. Will you still have some time to spend with your boys this weekend?"

She laughed at him. "Saturdays, young men have their own agendas. Or don't you remember the other side of twenty? Tomorrow, though, they'll take me out for brunch. We splurge on double-yolk omelets once a month."

Matt smiled, glad to see her beaming with pride. Before too many years, the boys would be applying to colleges. He'd have to look into scholarship possibilities then, or maybe a private grant.

"Have fun tomorrow then. You can leave as soon as you've given Abby the lowdown. Tell her to wait for me. She can keep herself busy reading clients' files until I get here."

As Matt waited for the elevator, he thought again about Abby. Or maybe it was just a continuation of one long thought that had extended over nearly two days. He would probably be back in the office by five o'clock. By then he would have to come up with a safe method of relating to her. Last night, as he had drifted off to sleep, she had come to him. Those lovely limbs, mocha eyes, the tumble of red hair curling down over her shoulders…amazing.

Now he firmly assured himself that, once they buckled down to a regular work schedule, he would discover enough irritating things about her to shut down his rogue hormones. Then he'd have no more of *those* thoughts.

Abby was a little surprised that Wanda Evans, her boss at the Cup and Saucer, took her sudden resignation as calmly as she did. "Don't you worry, dear, I have everything covered here. This sounds like a wonderful opportunity. Good luck." And that was that.

Her arrival at Smythe International was unremarkable, too. She was met by Paula Shapiro, the woman she'd seen with Matt the day before. Paula introduced herself, with a twinkle in her eyes. "My official title is executive assistant. Plain old secretary would be fine by me. My real job is to keep the man from killing himself and the rest of us with work."

Abby laughed a little nervously. "He does seem to like getting things done fast…and his own way."

"Oh, he knows his own mind, that's for sure. And there's both heaven and hell to pay when he doesn't get it. But let me tell you," Paula whispered confidentially as she took Abby's arm and guided her past two empty offices then into a quiet conference room, "the best way to handle the man is not to let him think you're afraid of him. He knows enough not to mess with me, but he scared off his last four hostesses without even realizing he was doing it. Before that, one fell in love with him and, of course, that was the kiss of death as far as Matt is concerned. He keeps business strictly separate from his social life. And the one before that, she got herself engaged to one of his clients and flew off to Paris with him.''

Abby shook her head. This didn't sound encouraging at all. "I'm curious…how long has each of his hostesses before me lasted?''

"The longest was a year. The shortest, two weeks. I'm hoping you'll hang in with us a while.'' Paula squeezed her arm and waved toward a seat at the long mahogany table piled with tabbed folders. "We could use some stability around here. It's hard having to work with new people all the time.''

Abby smiled with more confidence than she felt. "I may take my time making a decision, but I don't scare easily.''

"Good, then let's get to work. I'll start by filling you in on the people you'll be meeting in New York.''

They reviewed several files then moved on to basic information about the company's other offices and details of her job. At four-thirty Paula looked at her watch. "I have to go now, but Matthew asked that you wait for him. You might want to start reading through the correspondence in the Miller and Capshaw files.''

"Do you think he'll be long?'' Abby asked. Accustomed to early suppers, she was already feeling a little hungry.

Paula shrugged. "He's unpredictable, but I expect he'll show up within an hour or so.''

Abby nodded. An hour would be easy to kill. After her new boss dismissed her for the evening, she'd buy a pizza with everything on it and share it with Dee to celebrate her new job. Meanwhile, there was a lot to learn.

Sometime later, Abby rubbed her tired eyes and looked up at the clock on the conference room wall. It was six forty-five. She started hunting through cabinets and drawers, hoping to find a forgotten Twinkie or apple, but there was nothing. Her stomach was rumbling impatiently. Abby considered raiding the bountifully stocked storage rooms, but feared there might be rules against employees snacking on the entertainment supplies. There were several restaurants nearby, but not the kind that delivered. Her orders had been to wait for her boss's return. It would be just her luck for him to show up while she was out getting dinner. And so she waited, with growing irritation.

By half past seven, she was starving, furious and wishing she had learned how to swear. Matt had a cell phone in his car. She'd seen it, damn it! All he had to do was pick it up and let her know she would be working through the dinner hour so she could run out and grab a sandwich. She searched Paula's desktop for his phone number, but his assistant didn't keep a Rolodex. The drawers were all locked. If her telephone list was on her computer, it would be secured by a password.

Growing desperate, Abby put all the files away then let herself into Matt's office. He must keep a record somewhere of his contact numbers, she reasoned. Flicking on a light, she walked in. There were no file cabinets in this room, just one enormous desk that looked as if it was made of an exotic type of wood with ebony inserts at the corners, a masculine style of chair and two visitors' chairs shoved into corners of the room. The only other item in the room was an oriental carpet in rich golds and blues, covering the expanse of polished wood floor between door and desk. Smythe kept things simple but certainly wasn't concerned with overspending.

Abby walked over to his desk. On the leather blotter lay a neat stack of unopened mail and, alongside, an ivory-handled letter opener embossed with a family crest. His family's?

Idly, she flipped through the envelopes. One caught her eye. Or, at least, the name of the recipient printed on its front did. Lord Matthew Robert Smythe, seventh earl of Brighton.

Abby brushed her fingertips across the creamy vellum.

The return address was London, England. An attorney's office, it appeared. She wondered why Matt had come to America to start and run his company, when all of his family ties were in Britain. He spoke with only a slight accent, and she'd sensed, more than once, that he didn't like people to use his aristocratic title. It seemed so very strange, almost as if he was intentionally erasing his past. *Why?* she wondered. *Was it just a privacy issue—or something more important?*

Abby shook her head, annoyed with herself. After all, there was no reason for her to care at all about her new boss's personal quirks. *Or was there?* she wondered as she moved back out of his office. If he simply eliminated people and places that bothered him or were no longer of use to him, where did that leave her or any other employee?

Maybe Paula hadn't been entirely truthful about the women who had taken this job before her. Maybe they had left because Matt had done something to drive them away, or had fired them. If this was so, a few months from now she might end up the same way. Dropped in the middle of New York City, Los Angeles or Hong Kong, without a job or a way to get home to her safe, predictable Chicago.

The thought chilled her, then infuriated her. Abby shot another glance at the clock. It was almost 8:00 p.m. Slinging her purse over one shoulder, she shut off the lights and locked the office door behind her. Why was she waiting around for a man who didn't have the decency to consider his employees' welfare?

Matt strode into the marble-and-glass lobby and had started past the security guard when the man in the glass booth stopped him with a wave. "Hold up there, Lord Smythe. A young lady left a note for you."

"Young lady?" Matt had to think for a moment before deciding he could only mean Abby. He grabbed the slip of paper and kept on moving into the waiting elevator. Before he reached his floor, he had finished the note and cursed females everywhere. The elevator doors opened, he hit the Lobby button and rode back down to the foyer.

Matt was still fuming by the time he reached Abby's apartment building in Chicago's famous Loop area. A man with an armload of groceries had just buzzed himself in. Without breaking stride, Matt followed him through the door. The mailboxes were labeled with tenants' names and apartment numbers. There was no elevator that he could see; he took the metal stairs in twos, his rage mounting with each flight. He found Apartment 4B and pounded a clenched fist on the door, knocking leaves from a dried floral wreath onto the floor.

Abby cracked open the door and stared at him over the crust of a grilled cheese sandwich halfway into her mouth. "What are—"

"Why are you *here?*" he interrupted with his own question. Not waiting to be asked in, he marched past her into the little apartment. "Can't you understand a simple directive? 'Wait for me until I return.' Or wasn't Paula clear on that?"

Abby stood at the open doorway, staring at him as if he were a rogue moose that had just wandered in off the city street and into her living room. "You have atrocious manners."

"Never mind my etiquette," he growled. "I intended to review some important material with you tonight."

"I stayed more than a reasonable length of time," she retorted, kicking the door closed behind her. "It was well past normal work hours, and on a Saturday besides. I was starving, there was no food around and I had no way of contacting you. For all I knew, you'd totally forgotten about me. I might have been there all night."

Matt winced. Had he really been that thoughtless? He had planned on taking Abby out to a working dinner. He wasn't accustomed to eating his last meal of the day until eight or nine o'clock in the evening, and it hadn't occurred to him that her body clock might function differently than his. But he wasn't about to let her off the hook so easily.

"You're on twenty-four-hour call for this job, Ms. Benton."

"No," she said crisply, "I am not." She took another bite, chewed and swallowed, all the while fixing him with a cool gaze. ''I need my sleep, my meals and some order in my life. I'll work hard for you, but I have to know what to expect so that I can take care of my personal requirements. I won't sit around an empty office, twiddling my thumbs and starving while I wait on your beck and call.''

Matt glared at her, feeling heat rise from beneath his collar. *Not even Paula spoke to him like this— without the respect he was due as a British royal, a man who had made millions, a man who—*

He blinked, shocked at the words that had tumbled through his mind. Whose voice had *that* been? Not his own. Respect—the old earl, his father, had gone on endlessly about it, all through Matt's childhood.

In fact, the family's prominence in society had been so important to Matthew's father, the earl of Suffolk had skirted convention. The accepted rules of peerage dictated that his eldest son should hold the next lower title to his own, that of viscount, leaving his two younger sons simply as lords. But generations of Smythes, by marrying with other aristocratic families, had collected a fine list of titles not, in the old earl's opinion, to be wasted. He'd elected that his sons should also be honored as earls, though of regions of lesser historical importance than his own. Nobody had yet dared challenge the man since all the titles were legitimate. And so, incredibly, they were a family of four earls.

Distant echoes of a troubled and lonely past washed over him. He was stunned. Of all the men in the world, the one he least wanted to emulate was the earl of Suffolk.

Abby was still speaking. He tried to clear his mind and focus on her words.

"...and after I finish eating, I'll have to think a little more about accepting this job *as your personal slave.*" Her eyes flashed in challenge at him.

He bit down on his lower lip to keep from laughing. Is that how he came off? The tyrannical slaveholder? Now that he gave it some thought, he had been rather inconsiderate not to at least call and make sure his plans suited her.

"I, um, I apologize," he said haltingly, watching her polish off the last nibble of her sandwich.

"I should think so," she agreed, licking buttery crumbs from her fingertips.

"I tend to work from the moment I wake to the second my head hits the pillow, catching meals where I can. I suppose I assume others do the same."

"Don't get me wrong," she said. "I can work as fiercely as anyone. But I tend to fall apart if I don't get a meal now and then."

He chuckled. "Wouldn't want that, would we? Your falling apart." She was so nicely put together, after all.

Abby shrugged. "Perhaps your other assistants died of malnutrition."

He laughed out loud this time. She had a sense of humor, as well as spunk! "Hardly. I'm not exactly sure why they left. Actually, some I didn't mind seeing go. They weren't anywhere as good as you are with people."

Abby allowed him a tentative smile. He'd meant to flatter her, but it hadn't been a lie. She *was* good. Very good. He had seen his guests respond to her open friendliness. Matt stepped closer to her, feeling an inexplicable need to lessen the space between them.

"In my own defense, I had planned to take you out for dinner at a restaurant not far from the office. They have a quiet table near the back where I thought we might finish our business day in a more pleasant atmosphere than at the office."

"Oh." She looked suddenly deflated.

"We can still go. Maybe you could consider that sandwich an appetizer?" The idea of sitting across a table from her, the glow from a candle stuck in a Chianti bottle lighting her pretty face, suddenly appealed to him immensely.

She shook her head but didn't seem to have her heart in turning down his invitation. "I'm pretty tired. Is there some other way we can prepare for the trip?"

"I'll call you tomorrow around ten in the morning, if that's all right. Perhaps a few details over the phone—travel information and such. The rest we can discuss on the plane, Monday. I'll bring your contract with me, and you can look it over and sign it then."

"Good," she said. "Thank you."

He hovered over her for a moment longer. The urge to kiss her had been building since he had walked into her apartment. The impulse was strong...but all wrong, he told himself. Instead, he extended his hand to shake hers. A poor substitute, but there it was.

"Thank you for taking the job," he said. "I'll try to see that you won't regret it."

# Three

———

**T**wo days later, Abby stepped from the private elevator into the Fifth Avenue penthouse and looked around, her heart thumping with excitement. Matthew Smythe's New York digs were professionally decorated entirely in black and white. No in-between shades of gray, no colors. The decor, she decided, suited his personality perfectly. Black or white, yes or no…never a maybe.

Black onyx tiles alternated with white marble, leading from the foyer into the living room. Sophisticated nude female sculptures in pristine white alabaster flanked the wide doorway opening into the suite. The carpeting was a creamy Berber. Bookending an immense glass table, set low enough for drinks or to serve a light meal, were a pair of black leather sofas. Fresh flowers overflowed twin vases at the ends of the fireplace mantle, but every bloom of lily, rose and baby's breath was pure white.

However, Abby had little time to muse over her boss's taste in decor. The folder she held contained their itinerary for the next ten days, and there was barely time to breathe between meetings.

"As I explained, I keep a second suite of rooms entirely separate from mine, for my employees," Matt said, motioning absently toward a door as he reached for the telephone. "You'll have complete privacy and three rooms to choose from. Take your time unpacking and freshening up. I have several calls to make, then we'll take a car to the Haversfield meeting at three o'clock."

Abby nearly choked on a laugh but managed to hold it back. Take her time? He was giving her an entire thirty minutes. She had hoped for a shower to rinse off the airport dust, but there was no time for that now. She'd have to settle for a spritz of perfume, change of clothes and a few strategic touches with a curling iron.

While Abby hurriedly unpacked, her thoughts returned to the envelope she'd discovered on Matt's desk. No wonder he was used to getting his own way; he had undoubtedly been terribly spoiled as a child, raised in the lap of aristocratic luxury. No doubt his adoring parents had set him up in business in the States, she thought indignantly. Most people struggled just to pay their rent and buy groceries. This man's biggest worry was how many thousands he could add to his net worth on any given day! And he barely blinked when one employee left and another slipped into the vacant slot.

She had never liked self-involved people. When

she added wealth to the equation, the earl of Brighton seemed even less her type.

*So what?* she asked herself.

She hadn't taken the job because of Matthew Smythe's winning personality. Her reasons had been purely practical. And Matt wouldn't be disappointed when she left since none of his other hostesses had stayed as long.

There was only one problem. Despite his cavalier treatment of her, as if she were no more than an insignificant cog in his personal wheel of success, she was strongly attracted to him. And, she had noticed, she wasn't the only one. Everywhere they went, his mere presence commanded the attention of women. When he wanted a woman in his bed, she had no doubt there would be one. So, what did he want from *her?* A woman with no experience in pleasing a man. A woman who hadn't even been able to entice her fiancé those last few steps to the altar. The pain returned with sharp, accusing jabs to her heart. She took three deep breaths then forced herself to think only of business.

There was one meeting in Manhattan that afternoon and another that evening. As they approached the first prospective client, Matt clasped Abby's hand and casually rested it in the crook of his arm. He gave no other indication to the woman who represented the upscale, mail-order service that they might be more than boss and employee—no pet names, no suggestive touches. That one gesture, though, was enough to indicate an intimate connection.

Although Matt acted as if he didn't even feel her hand on his arm, Abby gave an unintended jump as her fingers curled around his suit sleeve. She was surprised to feel taut muscles in his biceps and forearm—something she hadn't noticed before. She would have thought he was too busy cutting million-dollar deals to exercise. Apparently he had found a way.

She imagined the rest of his body, just as toned and tight…and hard. Her knees felt rubbery. She managed to play her supporting role through the first meeting and not melt into a puddle of feminine desire every time he looked at her, but it was hard work.

"I entertain my foreign suppliers differently than my customers in the U.S.," Matt explained later that day as they rode to their dinner meeting at the Four Seasons.

The brilliant lights of Broadway and Times Square flashed past the limo's windows, and Abby felt suddenly breathless again. This was another kind of sexiness. A city could be sensual, edgy, provocative…although not as gut ticklingly so as a man like Matthew Smythe.

"Let me guess," she said, keeping her voice steady, her eyes on the view outside the car's windows. "Tonight the situation is reversed; they'll be trying to seduce you."

Matt gave her a strange look.

Abby winced. Why had she used *that* word? *Seduce.* It held dangerous multiple meanings. Maybe it was the allure of the city working on her subconscious. Or maybe it was because she couldn't stop thinking about her new boss in an unclothed sort of way…because of those hidden muscles she'd discovered.

"I suppose seduction is a good analogy." He gave her one more quick glance before returning to notes on his laptop, but didn't seem to notice her embarrassment. The computer was hooked to a modem, he had explained to her earlier, which allowed him to communicate with the touch of a few keys with any of his offices, as well as clients and suppliers around the world. "Tonight," he continued, "the vice-president of an Austrian company will be pitching his products to us. I already have a deal with a similar firm based in Munich, but I'm not satisfied with the quality of their goods."

"Then why are you entertaining him, instead of the other way around?"

After typing a few more sentences, Matt leaned back against the leather upholstery to observe her solemnly. "I never let anyone pay my way," he said. "It's one of my rules."

She frowned. "Why is that?"

"It just is." He shrugged as if it didn't really matter. But she sensed that this was an important issue to him. "Neither I nor anyone on my staff accepts gifts. If one of my clients should send you anything more than a tasteful bouquet of flowers, you're to send the gift back immediately, with your gracious thanks."

"I understand," she said, though she really didn't. She dismissed this as just another example of his eccentricity.

Dinner at the Four Seasons was sedately spectacular. The enormous reflection pool in the middle of the single spacious dining room caught the light from the ceiling above. All the seating faced the room's center, giving the room the feeling of a theater-in-the-round. The elegantly attired waiters took center stage. The couple sharing their table spoke only a little English and clearly preferred German, which Matt spoke fluently.

*"Ich spreche ein bitte,"* Abby apologized at the beginning of their conversation for the little she spoke. She remembered only a few phrases from her high school foreign language classes.

Matthew said something to his guests in German, then translated for her. "I told them you've only recently joined our firm." He laid a hand over hers on the tabletop, as if to demonstrate an additional personal nature to their relationship.

The message must have been lost to Frau Gremmel, a pretty blonde with wandering eyes. Her gaze hungrily took in the dashing waiters, then settled on Matt with special intensity. Impulsively, Abby turned her hand over, palm up, lacing her fingers through Matt's, as if tenderly marking her territory. She felt an answering tremor through his hand and knew she'd taken him by surprise. *Good,* she thought, *someone ought to shake up the man once in a while.*

He started to move his hand out of hers, but she closed her fingers around his. Not so hard that he couldn't pull away if he really wanted to, just enough to challenge him. Later, if he asked her what she'd been doing, she would say that she'd just been playing along. Secretly, it gave her almost as much satisfaction to rattle his cage as it did to disappoint the fair Frau.

For the life of him, Matt couldn't remember what he had ordered for dinner. He vaguely nodded as the waiter placed the sizzling roast duckling topped with mango chutney in front of him. His senses seemed to be reacting in slow motion. Staring at the food before him, he felt Abby release his hand to pick up her own fork and dig into a thick cut of rare prime rib glistening in its own juices. For a moment everything in the room seemed to wash away in a blue haze, and all he felt or knew was the sensation of cool air lifting the perspiration from his palm, where her hand had been.

Observing Abby's calm expression and cool tan-colored eyes as she took her first bite of the pink beef, he supposed that the simple gesture of cupping his hand in hers had meant less than nothing to her. But the knitting motion of their fingers and the silky touch of her skin had shaken him profoundly. The subtlest shift of her fingertips against his flesh had sent electrical shocks pinging through his wrist, up his arm. But *her* composure had been absolute.

Matt listened with only half an ear to Gremmel's glowing description of the wide range of confections his company offered. But his glance kept straying to the petite figure seated on his right. Abby was heavily into her beef, putting it away, bite by delicate bite but with great zeal.

Abby finished before any of them, but kept a lively conversation going until the others were done eating. "And how was your salmon, Frau Gremmel?" she asked politely.

*"Ganz gut. Danke,"* the woman answered.

"Herr Gremmel?" Matt asked, taking Abby's cue.

"This has been delightful, Lord Smythe. As my wife has said, most delicious. You must let us entertain you the next time you are in Vienna. You and your charming companion." He winked good-naturedly at Abby.

Matt smiled and nodded. Showing Abby around the elegant, old city appealed to him. But Austria also made him think of Thomas. His older brother lived most of the year in Elbia, just across the Austrian border. Matt had only briefly met his new bride and the children Thomas had inherited in the bargain. He was curious to see if marriage had changed the dedicated bachelor. It wasn't long ago that he would have a staked a fortune on none of the Smythe brothers marrying. But in the last year both Thomas and their younger brother, Christopher, had taken brides.

"Perhaps we will take you up on that offer," Matt said.

He let Gremmel put the icing on his sales pitch, then asked that samples be shipped to his home office. They parted with handshakes and polite wishes that they would soon be doing business for their mutual profit. Abby warmly added her own hopes for their safe travel home. She treated everyone as if they were family, he realized, amazed at how naturally she pulled off the quick hugs and cheek kisses.

On the way back to the hotel, Matt sat silently in the back of the limo while Abby chattered nonstop, still excited about all she'd learned at the dinner meeting. He gave her one-word answers when he could and tried to tune her out.

It wasn't that her enthusiasm annoyed him. Quite the opposite. He fed off of her euphoria. Her buoyant mood stimulated him in ways he didn't want to be stimulated at the moment. But he couldn't help thinking about her small hand resting on the seat between them. Couldn't help pondering how easy it would be for him to pick up her fingers and pull her across the seat toward him. Then he'd silence her lips with his own.

He hoped that by the time they took the elevator

up to the penthouse she would run out of steam. But she was still happily analyzing the evening, gleaning all she could from the experience, when they stepped across the marble threshold.

"Will you need me for anything more tonight?" she asked cheerfully.

The question jolted him. "*Need* you?"

"Yes. Do you want me to draw up notes about tonight's meeting before I call it a night?"

He glanced at the clock on the mantel. "It's after eleven o'clock. I think that can wait until morning."

"Good." She yawned, stretching her arms high over her head. The motion thinned out her already slender waist and lifted her breasts provocatively. "I'm exhausted. That meal *really* was wonderful, by the way."

"Yes, good...it was quite good," he muttered, hastily turning away. *Why did she unnerve him so?*

A moment later, he spun around, intending to ask her about the thing she'd done with their hands in the restaurant. But she was gone. He heard water running in her bathroom. Sighing, he shook his head.

Matt waited impatiently outside the door to her suite for the water to stop running. Why he waited, he wasn't sure. He heard her feet padding across the floor of the adjoining suite. She was humming to herself, sounding delightfully content and pleased with herself.

He stepped close to the door separating her private quarters from his domain. "Abby?"

The humming stopped. "Did you want me, Matt?"

"Yes." *Yes!* he thought wildly. *I want you out of those clothes and in my arms.* "Would you come in here for just a moment?"

There was a delay while he imagined her pulling a robe over her nightdress, then she appeared in the doorway. She had indeed put on a simple pink cotton robe. And it almost concealed the fact that she wore nothing beneath it. Unfortunately, her attempt at modesty failed to account for two crucial factors. The lamps in the room backlighted her figure, so that her long, slim legs showed through the fabric. And her nipples were raised, poking little brown dots through the pale cloth.

Matt swallowed, then swallowed again, his throat suddenly so dry he doubted he could speak. Her hair cascaded in poppy-red waves over her shoulders, and her eyes were soft, sleepy, and unafraid. The nervous energy of their earlier encounters was gone. She looked as if her only desire was to climb between two sheets and fall asleep fast. But he only wanted to get into bed…with her…definitely not to sleep.

"Yes?" she repeated.

He stepped closer. She smelled of bath soap, minty toothpaste and the fabric softener in her robe. A good clean country girl, he thought. He wanted to gather her to him, bury his face in her lush, damp red mane…inhale her, taste her.

"On second thought," he began hesitantly, "maybe you should jot down just a few notes before you go to bed. Include a few personal observations about the Gremmels—meal choices, their son's name, hobbies. I keep records of that sort of thing. You might forget by morning."

Abby looked puzzled. "All right."

She started to step back into her suite, but his hand shot out and closed around her wrist, stopping her.

He stared at his fingers as if they were mutinous employees, acting without his permission.

"Anything else?" she asked, her voice sounding husky. It sent a flash of heat through his body. Heat that settled low within him and simmered.

He might have snapped his hand back and said *no*. But as Abby turned toward him, the sweetness of her breath crossed his face, and he unwisely focused on her lips, softly parted. Her mocha eyes widened as they took in his expression.

Later, Matt realized that what happened next had been inevitable from the start. He pulled Abby into his arms and kissed her hard and long. He kept telling himself that at any moment she would let out a protesting screech, or, at the very least, shove him away. But she did neither. And without some negative response from her, he couldn't stop moving his lips over hers...couldn't stop teasing the corners of her sweet mouth with the tip of his tongue...couldn't stop drinking in her lovely essence.

She didn't exactly return his kiss, but she didn't reject it either. This intrigued him. Clearly, she wasn't a woman who gave herself over to every man who made a move on her. He had somehow known that from the moment she popped into his office that Friday afternoon. She was perky and playful, but could be serious when the occasion demanded. She wasn't a shallow flirt or a sleep-around girl, so why was she letting him get away with this?

It was impossible not to test her.

Keeping her lips busy, he slowly moved his hand between their bodies and cautiously rubbed his thumb across one nipple through her robe. She shuddered but didn't tell him to stop. He cupped her breast. She sighed lightly into his mouth. He kissed the line of her jaw, moved his lips down her throat, and dipped beneath the top edge of her robe. His tongue flicked deliciously over her bare nipple half a dozen times. It took another moment for his mind to register the gentle sounds coming from her throat and her sudden rigidity in his arms, as weak protests.

Releasing her, he watched with regret as she quickly tugged the neckline of her robe back into place. But not before he caught a delightful glimpse of white breast. She was utterly lovely. She even had freckles there. What fun it would be to try to lick them off...one by one.

"I'm sorry!" he blurted out, although he wasn't at all. "I don't know why I did that." He did know.

She stared at him, her cheeks flushed, her hands trembling and clutching her robe in a bunch under her throat. She was breathing hard. "I told you when I accepted this job—"

He could hear tears edging her trembling voice, and he was instantly sorry he had taken such liberties with her. What he had done was inexcusable, his libido be damned!

"Believe me," he said hastily, "this has never happened before. I never intended to use my position as your employer to force myself on—" He shook his head, amazed at how insincere he sounded, even to himself. She must think the very worst of him. "I'm terribly sorry, Abby. It won't happen again. I promise."

She gave him a mystifying look, then dropped her glance to the floor and wiggled her bare toes in the carpeting. "I hope I didn't do anything to encourage...you know—"

Now that she was trying to take some of the blame on herself, he felt somewhat relieved. "Don't even think that. I just reacted. I don't understand why." Of course he understood why. She was adorable! She was irresistible!

Abby drew a long, slow breath, then let it out and looked up at him shyly through rusty-red eyelashes. "And I don't understand why I didn't stop you sooner. I'm not usually so vulnerable. I even took a self-defense course." Her eyes sparkled mischievously. "Learned just where to kick a man."

"Thank you for not using your expertise." Matt smiled shakily at her. "I swear I'll be on good behavior from now on. Really."

Abby nodded, turned away, and stepped into the other suite, shutting the door quietly behind her. He heard the lock take hold with a firm click. Wise move, he thought—for even now he still ached for her.

Abby leaned against the backside of the door and let her forehead drop with a soft thud against the polished wood. "Don't try too hard to be a good boy, Matt," she whispered.

It took her a solid five minutes to regulate her breathing, stop trembling and make her way into the bedroom. She let the robe slip from her shoulders to the floor and stood very still in front of the mirrored closet doors, examining her own reflection. She could still feel the tingles aroused by the moist caresses of Matt's tongue across her breast. She quivered. A long, slow stream of heat coursed through her and she closed her eyes, enjoying it until the sensation spent itself out.

Opening her eyes, Abby veered quickly away from

the mirror and grabbed her flannel nightdress out of the dresser drawer. A few minutes earlier, she had put it away with the thought that it was too warm to wear that night. Now all that seemed to matter was completely covering her body.

As Abby lay in bed that night, she wished she hadn't flinched. She wished she hadn't let on that she was shocked, then Matt might have closed his warm mouth over her…and who knew what other wonderful experiences he might have introduced her to before the night was over. She was twenty-five years old and a virgin. Maybe that was the real reason she hadn't told him to stop.

Curiosity.

# Four

Abby was fascinated by New York City, but even more captivated by Matt. She loved the throbbing energy of Manhattan…the hard, gray buildings and immense polished brass doors that captured the sunlight…the sophisticated fashions displayed in the windows of Bloomingdale's, Saks Fifth Avenue and in the chic shops in spectacular Trump Tower. But Matt was an enigma, and that attracted her even more strongly toward him.

He demanded long hours, hard work and perfection from her. But to do her job effectively, she had to have free access to him, for there were dozens of decisions to be made in preparation for each of his meetings. Yet, after their steamy incident in the penthouse, he seemed to intentionally distance himself from her. Sometimes she wouldn't see him all day.

On the fourth day they were in the city, she decided

that she would have to do something to make him feel more comfortable around her. Bergdorf Goodman was on Fifth Avenue and 57th Street, right around the corner from their penthouse. The first chance Abby got, she bolted for the elegant women's clothing store. Abby passed by displays of elegantly sensual garments in lush colors of silk, her eyes skimming over beautiful dresses that she could now afford because of her generous clothing allowance. These would only make it more difficult for her and Matt to work together. The key, she decided, was playing down her appearance. Ultraconservative business clothing, that's what she needed to cool the sensual tension between the two of them.

Abby found two ideal outfits at the precise moment a sales associate spotted her. "That one and that one," she said, pointing. Fifteen minutes later she had tried them on and was on her way back to the hotel, pleased with her ingenuity.

Matt looked for the third time at his watch, then at the door to his employees' suite. It wasn't like Abby to be late for an appointment, but he refrained from knocking for fear she might breeze into the living room in her robe again. He couldn't handle that.

He considered a single, very dry martini, just to steady his nerves, then dismissed the need for liquid courage as ludicrous. What did he have to be nervous about?

The door opened, and there was his answer. *Her.*

Abby stepped into the room in a smart black-and-white suit. The collar of the jacket was high, a Mandarin style. The hem of the straight-cut skirt fell demurely below her calves, revealing only her ankles.

She smiled at him, and his eyes immediately went to her lips—not blazing red to compliment the sophistication of the suit, but a petal-soft pink. Her hair was pinned up in a tight chignon. She looked like a schoolmarm, dressed by *Vogue*.

"What the bloody hell is *that?*" he demanded.

She blinked at him. "I went shopping today. You don't think this is appropriate for tonight?"

It probably was suitable, he thought. She looked smart, elegant and very beautiful. What bothered him was the underlying intent of the outfit. She couldn't have covered another inch of her body, short of wearing a hooded sweatshirt and pants. Her motive was all too clear.

But the ploy worked in reverse. He found the high collar and sleek black silhouette provocative. A challenge. An invitation to remove every last thread from her body, to touch her, taste her, dishevel her.

"Take it off," he growled.

"Excuse me?" She was glaring at him, but also looking worried.

"Wear that poppy-red thing you had on the other night," he grumbled and went to the bar to mix the martini he'd earlier decided against.

"A cocktail dress? To a daytime meeting?"

"Something else then...not that thing." He didn't hear her leave the room, but thought she must have from the sudden silence in the room. When he turned around, she was still there, observing him coolly. "Well?" he demanded, sipping the clear, pungent liquid that burned its way down his throat.

"I know why you don't like this outfit and why you've been so difficult to pin down the last few days," she said.

He studied his drink. It could have used one of those little pearl onions. He tried to concentrate on that shortcoming. Anything to avoid meeting her eyes.

"Did you hear me, Matt?"

He sighed. "So enlighten me. Why don't I like the suit?"

"Because you want to sleep with me but you won't admit it."

His laugh was too loud and forced to be sincere. "Quite an imagination you have, lady."

"I don't think so," she said slowly, her eyes washing over him in an unsettlingly perceptive way. She stepped closer to him, and he had to brace himself from backing away defensively. "I think we're attracted to each other. But we have to find a way to work around those feelings. I can't do my job if you keep disappearing and won't communicate with me."

He nodded. "I see." He wasn't admitting anything except that he had made himself scarce the last few days. "Whether or not there's anything happening between the two of us," he said carefully, "dressing like the matron of a girl's boarding school isn't the answer."

"I'm just dressing conservatively."

He couldn't stand it any longer. She was too composed, too sure of herself…and he was falling apart inside. "Damn it, Abby, grow up! You could walk into this room in a bikini and I wouldn't lay a hand on you!"

She tilted her head to one side and observed him doubtfully. "I think I'll stick with this."

The following day Abby didn't have time to brief Matt on his messages until they were on their way to his afternoon appointment. All morning had been spent with his lawyer, drawing up the contract with a new exporter. Matt had asked her to read the contract and witness his signature. She was flattered that he still was giving her a chance to view the inner workings of his business, even though their original boss–employee relationship had lurched precariously into temporary intimacy.

Beneath the low-key tempo of their business days, an undeniable electricity still flashed between them. By the time they were driving back across the city in the limo, Abby felt as if her flesh was prickling from the back of her neck to the bottoms of her heels. Still she tried to concentrate on the work at hand, which was keeping Matt up to date on his e-mail and phone messages.

"This one, I couldn't figure out," she said, checking the page she'd printed before they left the hotel. "Here, look. It's from Scotland. Something about the Knight of Castle Donan?"

He took the slip of paper from her with a laugh.

"It's from my brother Christopher. When we were boys we communicated in code, in the foolish hope my father wouldn't know what we were up to. Christopher was the Knight of Donan, one of the family properties that was passed on to him. He and his bride live in the castle now." He was reading while he was talking, but his smile gradually faded.

"Is something wrong?"

Matt leaned back into his seat, and she could see the muscles in his handsome face tighten with anxiety. "Nothing that hasn't been wrong for all of our lives."

Abby laid a hand over his as he crumpled the paper in his fist. "Can I help?"

"Not unless you can talk my brother out of a disaster in the making."

"What does he want to do?"

"Arrange a family reunion, at my father's estate."

Abby shook her head, confused. "Why is that a bad idea?"

"Because my father could give a damn about seeing any of us."

Abby stared at him. What a horrid way to feel, she thought. She waited patiently for more of an explanation. Eventually, Matt's anger seemed to subside.

"I'm sorry, this isn't your concern. Families can be so difficult." He looked at her. "Of course, growing up in a loving brood on your Illinois farm, you wouldn't understand. You've probably never had someone important to you walk out of your life when you needed them most."

She stared at Matt, understanding in that precious moment that he'd revealed something to her he probably hadn't meant to. "Your father left you and your brothers?" she asked gently.

"No," he said tightly, "my mother. She left my father and us three boys without a word of explanation. The earl didn't know what to do with us. Packed us off to boarding school as soon as each of us turned six. Until then there were nannies. We rarely saw him."

Abby chewed her bottom lip sympathetically. Such a cold childhood. "So Christopher lives in Scotland?"

"Yes, he's the youngest. Just married an American woman. They're restoring the castle. My older brother, Thomas, told me she's a stunning woman and he was right. She's very good to Christopher's daughter, too. Actually, I haven't seen either of my brothers in over a year.''

''And your father?''

''I haven't seen him since I left England when I turned twenty-one.''

She gasped. ''Over ten years!''

His jaw locked. ''Don't look at me like that. The man ignored me all my life. Why should I make an effort to play the doting son now? Besides, if he wanted to see me, he's perfectly capable of booking a flight and coming here. He has more money than he knows what to do with, and he's in good health.''

Despite the tough front Matt was putting up, Abby sensed his pain. ''Pride sometimes interferes with our speaking our real feelings.''

''What's that supposed to mean?'' he barked.

''I just meant, your father might want to tell you that he loves you and is proud of you…he just doesn't know how.''

Matt's face clouded again with anger. But just as quickly his expression softened as he looked down at their hands, hers resting over his. ''I'd like to think that. It's just difficult to believe, after all this time—'' He broke off, his voice choked with emotion. ''I remember her.''

''Your mother?''

He nodded. ''I was very young, but I remember how beautiful and soft she was. How her face glowed when she bent down to take me in her arms. She was everything he was not. Tender, affectionate, playful.''

The limo rolled on, past the Broadway billboards and onto 58th Street. Abby wished they had the entire night to talk like this. She felt so close to Matt, on the verge of breaking down walls and understanding who the man was behind the tough shell of the international executive.

The question came to her, as it must often have come to Matt—if Lady Smythe had loved her children so dearly, why had she left them? He must have seen the question in her eyes.

"For the longest time, I was sure she had gone on holiday. Just forgotten to tell us that she was off to Cannes or Biarritz. But the months became years, and my father refused to speak her name or tell us anything about her reasons for leaving or where she might be."

"I'm so sorry, Matt," she whispered, over the fist-sized lump in her throat. She could hardly imagine the depth of his pain.

"I decided as soon as I was old enough, I would leave England and never go back. I'm at peace with myself now. I keep busy. I—" He broke off and looked out the window, and she could tell he was struggling for control of his emotions.

"Did you ever try to find her?" she asked.

He shook his head, unable to speak. He wanted to ask her to please stop talking now. He didn't want to talk. Not about this. Not about the darkest part of his life. But he couldn't even manage those few words.

For years, he'd have given anything to find a way to block out the pain. But there had never been a business coup perfect enough, or a person who touched his life deeply enough, to make the bitter past go away.

But here was Abby, sitting patiently beside him. Her warmth passed through the air between them, and the touch of her fingers lightly on his hand was soothing. The past didn't leave, but it felt somehow easier to bear.

Reaching up, she stroked the side of his cheek. He turned into her hand. She was an angel.

Matt sensed that he was moving toward her without any conscious effort. The space between them shrank by inches, until he was looking into her pretty eyes, until they were too close to be proper for any but lovers.

"I can't tell you why people leave," she whispered. "But they do. Even when they love us, or we believe they do...they leave."

He frowned. What was she telling him? That she too had been abandoned by someone? Not her parents. She'd told him they still lived outside of Chicago. A man, he thought. Someone she'd cared for had hurt her profoundly.

He wasn't aware of the final subtle movement that brought their lips together. But there they were, suddenly, touching...and the effect was like fire racing through his veins. He forgot about the driver on the other side of the privacy screen, forgot about the city, about appointments and deals and profit ratios. The world outside the limo no longer existed.

He pulled Abby to him. She willingly pressed into his chest and returned his kiss with sweet fervor. She tasted like honey and unshed tears—sweet and salty in the same moment. Raking his fingers through her hair, he tugged her head back to kiss her throat. She moaned low, and he felt the vibrations of her pleasure against his lips.

"I wish...I wish," he gasped between kisses.

"Yes?" she murmured dreamily.

"What are the chances we could cancel this meeting with...I can't even think of the man's name now." He laughed, irritated with himself for feeling utterly powerless.

"It's too late." Too late, she thought, for a lot of things. Like stopping the rush of emotions that had engulfed her.

He kissed her once, twice, three times on the lips quickly, stroked her wrists, her throat, swept tendrils of hair away from her misty eyes. "Tonight. After this is over. We are going to continue this."

She started to open her mouth, not to protest, but to ask him if he was sure this was what he wanted, because she wasn't sure of anything in her own mind or heart. He silenced her with another kiss before she could say a word.

"I've never needed anyone," he said solemnly. "Do you understand that, Abby? Never. But I need you now, if you are willing. I promise, this won't change a thing about our working together. I'll make it right. Don't be afraid."

"I'm not afraid," she said truthfully. Abby framed his strong face with her palms, brought him closer again, and kissed him firmly on the mouth. Suddenly, she knew. "I want you, too."

Abby thought the meeting that night would never end. The woman, who was marketing director of a large French vineyard, enjoyed long, leisurely dinners and wanted to talk about every aspect of Matt's business. There had been no way to cut the evening short.

On the way back to the hotel in the limo, Matt and Abby sat far apart on the leather bench, as if by mutual agreement. Abby was sure if she touched him at all, they both would spontaneously ignite. Besides, she needed time to think, time to plan how to tell him that she was a virgin before they reached a bed. But by the time they stood elbow to elbow in the elevator, she still hadn't found words that didn't sound foolish to her.

Matt unlocked the suite's door and stood back to let her inside. She turned toward him, desperate. What if her confession turned him off completely? He tossed his briefcase and jacket on a chair and took her into his arms before she could utter a single syllable. His mouth crushed over hers.

"I didn't hear a word that woman said all night," he groaned.

She gasped. "Matt, wait!" The room spun.

"I know…we have to talk about a few things." He was already unzipping the back of her dress. His hands slipped inside and found her bare waist. "I don't want you to be afraid. I've been very careful in the past. What about you?"

"No, oh no," she said quickly. "I've had boyfriends of course, but we've just been—" If he hadn't interrupted her, she would have said, *friends*.

"You don't have to justify anything to me," he said, kissing her cheek, her chin, her throat. "I know you aren't the type of woman who has been promiscuous or careless."

"That's not what I mean!" She felt frantic. "I was engaged once, but we…he didn't—" He was touching her in magical ways. It was impossible to think clearly.

"Nothing and no one before this night exists for us," he murmured in her ear, giving it a passing nibble. His hands expertly slid her dress off her shoulders and it dropped to her ankles. "I'll make you forget other men ever existed."

Part of her longed for that possibility. To finally and totally forget Richard would erase the most painful episode of her life.

Abby gazed up at Matt, shivering at the touch of his hot hands, seeking words that eluded her as her mind grew pleasantly misty. He unhooked her bra, let it drop to the floor, then quickly ripped off his necktie and dress shirt. Naked, but for the thin strip of lace and silk underwear at her hips, she forced out a few words. "You're going…to be…disappointed."

He laughed a sexy, throaty laugh as he quickly unzipped his pants and walked out of them. "I seriously doubt that, my dear." His eyes were afire with passion. He was moving far too fast for her. Clothing outsped words. Suddenly, he was lifting her in his arms and striding through the doorway, into his bedroom.

They fell as one onto the bed. He stretched out alongside her, his entire body rigid with sexual tension. He still wore tight briefs, but she could feel hard evidence of his arousal through the fabric, against her thigh. She sighed against his lips and relished the flavor of his long, potent kiss. His hands caressed her arms, shoulders, breasts…and she welcomed every sensation even as she chastised herself for her silence.

When he lifted his head to breathe between kisses, she drew a quick breath and pressed gently back against his chest. "Matt."

He smiled down at her. "Moving too fast for you, love?"

"Yes…no!" She gulped. "There's something you don't understand."

"About you?" He grinned wickedly. "So teach me." He was brushing his lips across the sensitive hollow of her throat, then his warm mouth lowered, covering her nipple. Whimpering, she squirmed with delight and agony. She didn't want him to stop, but he must understand what she was giving up for him, and not expect too much from her this first time.

The words exploded from her lips. "Richard left me because I wouldn't sleep with him."

Matt turned his head to one side and rested his cheek on her breast. His eyes darkened. "Who was Richard?"

"My fiancé."

He thought for a moment before coming up with the logical connection. "You wanted to wait for your wedding night?" He could understand that. But he imagined good old Dick might have felt pretty frustrated, knowing his bride had let others into her bed. Unless...

He looked across the pillow at her. "You're not saying that you're still a virgin, are you?"

She swallowed, nodded. Her eyes were enormous and full of fear. No wonder, he thought. Here he'd stripped the woman naked, flung her onto his bed, and was well into the delightful process of ravishing her. And this was her first time, ever. A low, primordial groan escaped from deep within him.

"You're disappointed, I know," she said quickly. "I don't have any experience, but I'll try. I will." Her eyes were brimming with tears and they wrenched at his heart. *What an insensitive jerk you are, Smythe!* he thought.

Matt rolled away from her on the bed, putting air between them. "What you're saying is...you've stayed a virgin all this time, by choice, until you marry. But now you're willing to sleep with me without any promise of a future?''

She lifted her chin slowly. "Yes," she said in a quiet but firm voice.

"Why?"

"I'm not sure…"

He felt a sudden flash of anger. What sort of game was she playing? Did this have to do with money? Or power? Or was she really as naïve as she sounded? "It's important," he said through gritted teeth. "Think about it, Abby. I don't want to hurt you, and I don't want you hating me in the morning."

"I wouldn't, I swear."

"Then why *now?* Why *me?*"

She swallowed, her heart in her throat as she reached behind her to the bedpost where Matt's robe hung. She modestly pulled it over her.

"When I was in college," she began, "I was friends with a group of six other girls. We were different. We didn't drink heavily or sleep around. In fact, we decided to make a pledge to remain virgins until we met and married the men of our dreams." She shrugged, feeling silly. She tried to explain further, but the words sounded like something out of a bad novel.

"I don't think that's terrible at all," Matt whispered, brushing the hair back from her eyes, his expression softer, the anger gone.

"At the time, it seemed very sensible, even romantic." Abby nibbled her lower lip thoughtfully. "I explained to the young men I dated that I wasn't into sex. Some never called again, which I accepted. Others stayed around for a while. Richard was patient for the longest time, and when he proposed I believed he would be the one.''

"Did you love him?''

"I thought I did. He was smart, kind and good-looking. He always treated me well.''

"But he didn't hang around for the wedding vows?''

She shook her head. "I stuck to my promise to myself—not until my wedding night. Two weeks before the ceremony, Richard totally lost it. He said he was fed up with my excuses. He demanded I prove that I loved him. He said that he loved me but wouldn't commit himself to marriage with a frigid woman who—''

"He called you that? Frigid?''

"Yes.'' She was crying now. Big sloppy, hiccupping sobs. "I understood then that I'd let him down. I'd been lying to both of us all along because I didn't really *want* to be intimate with him. I honestly felt nothing for the man that approached passion. But we had become best friends, and I wanted to keep him in my life. Marriage seemed the way to do it.''

Matt stared at her. "I can't believe anyone could think you a cold woman.'' He reached out and stroked the length of her bare arm.

She brushed his hand away. "What kind of woman turns down the man she's going to marry?'' she sobbed.

"No, Abby.'' His voice was tender. "You didn't turn him away, he left on his own. If he had loved you, he would have stayed. He wouldn't have needed proof.''

She was trembling violently, but he reached out

and stroked her cheek with a single finger, and the quaking gentled.

"He would have waited, then on your wedding night taught you to enjoy a man's body and believe in the magic of your own."

She looked up, as fragile as a tiny bird that had miraculously survived a hurricane. "I don't want to wait any longer," she whispered.

Matt felt as if the room had suddenly tipped sideways. He and everything in it were sliding off the edge into a void. What the hell was she asking of him?

"I'm twenty-five," she said before he could respond. "What if the man of my dreams never shows up? Suddenly, I'll be thirty-five...forty...or older." She looked at him sharply. "What are you smiling at?"

He gave her a wicked look, lay back on the bed and laced his fingers behind his head. "I'd say the very fact you're worried you might not get a chance to have sex proves you're a passionate woman at heart, and Richard was an idiot."

Her eyes widened, then she giggled. "Really?"

"Really."

He observed her, amused by the way her eyes kept shyly darting along the length of his body. She couldn't possibly miss how aroused he was. But he tried to ignore his body and consider what was best for her.

Abruptly, he rolled off the bed and stood beside it, looking down at her. "Any man who loved you would wait. Never doubt that, Abby."

He reached for a blanket at the foot of the bed,

covered her with it, then retrieved his robe from underneath.

"Where are you going?" she asked, her eyes wide with panic.

"The other room. You can sleep here if you like."

"But I thought you wanted to—"

"What I want and what is right are two separate issues, Abby." How the words stung him, as true as they were.

"No! No, you don't understand!" She sat up on the bed, the blanket pulled tightly against her breasts. "I *want* to have sex with you. I do!"

Matt shook his head and touched one fingertip to the tip of her nose. "Hormones talking. If there's one thing I've learned from the business world, it's to stick to first decisions. Don't let others change your mind."

"But this isn't *business!*" she cried in exasperation. "I want you to teach me everything about intimacy between a man and a woman. I want to know how it all works and feels and why people in movies look as if they're in pain at the same time they're obviously in ecstasy." Her eyes were clear and bright, and her blanket had dropped two inches, just enough to reveal a pair of lovely, brown nipples.

Matt felt helpless. He would have given anything to do as she asked. He had thought of nothing but Abby—about her body, about making love to her— for days. But he wasn't going to let it happen.

"Don't give up on your principles," he said gently. "Your perfect man, your husband may be just around the corner. Don't waste your virginity on me or any man who isn't willing to give you what you need, Abby."

She sat in the middle of the bed, watching help-lessly as Matt walked out of the room. All she could think was—for the second time in her life, she had driven away a man she really cared about. There was only one difference. This time, she hungered for him.

# Five

Abby felt like a small child who sees a full cookie jar on the kitchen counter, but is told she can't have chocolate chips before dinner for fear of spoiling her appetite. At one time she had believed the most precious gift she could give the man she married was her untouched body. It would be her promise to him of her love, trust and fidelity.

She wasn't sure why Matt was the man who made her want to abandon that dream. Why he should be trusted when others hadn't been? Did it have something to do with the amazing energy that had pulsed between them that first evening? No man had ever affected her that way before. And since then, she had only become more attracted to him.

"Abby, are you busy?" *his* voice interrupted her thoughts from the other side of her suite door.

She looked up from the desk where she sat, working on clients' files and their meeting schedule but making little progress. "No. Come in."

A sting of regret zapped through her as she looked up to see Matt walk through the door—tall, fit, eyes dark and intensely sharp. It had been two days since their aborted affair. She had felt his rejection deeply and tried to lose herself in their work, but had failed miserably.

Abby put on a polite smile of greeting. "I was just going over tomorrow's itinerary."

"Forget about that," he said decisively. "We're flying straight to Bermuda tomorrow morning."

She felt something tighten within her. Matthew Smythe wasn't a man who acted on impulse. Why the change of plans? "What about your remaining meetings in New York?"

"We'll reschedule for next month."

She frowned. "I didn't pack anything for a tropical climate."

"You can buy what you need once we get there. I've made the reservations. All you need to do is pack."

Matt stood in front of the plateglass windows overlooking Manhattan. He stared out at the skyline, wondering what he was getting himself into. But he'd made his decision and now he would follow through with it.

The phone rang, and he automatically picked it up before Abby could take the call. As he'd expected, it was Paula calling from Chicago.

"I got your message," she said. "What's this about your not coming back to headquarters for another week or more?"

"We're heading out to Bermuda."

"But your meetings—"

"Make my apologies and reschedule," he ordered impatiently.

"Yes, sir."

"Sorry, I didn't mean to snap."

"Yes, you did, but I forgive you," Paula said with exaggerated sweetness before she hung up.

Matt sighed. Paula might sometimes scold him for his insensitivity. But he knew, when he put his mind to it, that he was capable of putting others' needs ahead of his own. Now he was going to give his attention to Abby, because, he'd decided, she deserved his help.

The other side of the truth was, he had felt something intense, wonderful, and intriguing for Abby from the moment they'd met. And now an inner voice asked: *Why should you step aside for another man who will appreciate her less than you do?*

If Abby really meant what she had said, about wanting to lose her virginity, why should he stand in her way? The gentlemanly thing to do was to show her what she wished to learn. It would be purely an educational process, he reasoned. One that would benefit her later in life. She wouldn't be so apt to settle for a husband who couldn't satisfy her. She wouldn't settle for less than she deserved in a man.

But he would give her a few days to think over her decision, once they reached Hamilton, to make sure it wasn't an impetuous declaration. If she didn't change her mind, Smythe's Roost, just east of Hamilton, would be the perfect setting for her initiation into womanhood.

* * *

Bermuda's coves were bluer, her beaches pinker, her air sweeter smelling, and the island was, on the whole, far more enchanting than Abby could have imagined. The little pastel houses, piled up on the low verdant hills above aquamarine coves, ranged from luscious coral shades to soft turquoise. Slate rooftops, deeply ridged and coated with white lime to collect rainwater, gleamed in the sunlight. Soaring royal palms, Norfolk Island pines and new plantings of the beloved cedars once cherished by ancient shipbuilders, were interwoven with the richly scented blossoms of hibiscus, bougainvillea and morning glories. Tiny, porcelain-bright tree frogs whistled from the bushes, and an abundance of birds sang joyfully. Abby fell in love with the place immediately.

A car met them at the airport on the east end of the island and whisked them across causeways bridging the dozens of large and small islands that comprised the British Commonwealth known as Bermuda. Abby drew a quick breath when they pulled into a curving drive. At its end was a structure that resembled a pale green castle. "Oh my…this is it?"

"Smythe's Roost. Do you like it?"

"It's beautiful." Her eyes swept the gardens surrounding the house, lush with palm trees, exotic shrubs and flowering plants she couldn't identify. It was a pity Matt kept such a tight business itinerary. She'd have loved to wander the grounds leisurely, hike down to Hamilton, which he had told her was just a fifteen-minute walk, and explore some of the jewel-like coves she'd seen as the plane made its approach to land.

He must have read her mind. "This time you don't have to rush to change for our first meeting."

"Oh?" She quirked a brow at him. "Don't tell me you've built in an entire hour of freedom for your hostess?"

He smiled mysteriously. "Our first guests don't arrive for four days."

She turned to study his expression as the car pulled to a stop in front of a graceful veranda. "You're serious."

"Absolutely."

"Does Paula have any idea that you're not going to be working for four whole days?"

He laughed. There was a sexy, teasing tone to the sound that both thrilled and worried her. "Who says I won't be working?"

Abby stared at him and only moved from the back seat when the driver came around and opened the door for her. Something, she decided, was definitely different about Matthew Smythe. Although it probably had nothing to do with her, it worried her. After all, her living depended upon him. Just when she was getting used to the workaholic and tough taskmaster, was he developing a streak of playfulness? This couldn't be good.

Matt finished briefing his house staff. He knew he could trust them to have everything in order by the time his guests arrived at the end of the week. In the meantime, he intended to focus on Abby.

After arranging with Maria, his cook, for a light supper on the veranda, he went in search of Abby and found her sitting on a wooden bench at the far end of the garden, overlooking the cove. Sailboats tacked across sparkling blue-green water, while snorkelers took advantage of the last few hours of evening light to investigate submerged coral where tropical fish swam in abundance. Her red hair fell loosely around her shoulders, catching the sunlight.

"Pretty view," he commented.

She jumped and turned at the same moment. "I didn't hear you coming."

"Sorry, didn't meant to frighten you." He stopped close behind her and inhaled, catching a whiff of her scent above the natural perfume of the garden. "Ready for something to eat?"

"I'm famished," she admitted.

He offered his arm, and she hesitated only a moment before lightly tucking her fingers in its crook. They dined on the stone patio, sampling island dishes—conch prepared in a sweet papaya sauce, fresh fruit, potato rolls and coffee with a touch of cinnamon in it. He felt as nervous as a teenage boy, bucking up his courage to ask a girl out for their first date. He waited until they had finished eating and Abby leaned back in the white wicker chair to admire the sunset. Then he began the speech he'd been practicing all day.

"I have an idea I'd like to run past you, Abby."

"Moving corporate headquarters to Bermuda?" She grinned. "Fine with me."

"No. It involves your personal, rather than professional life."

She gazed at him solemnly across the table. "I didn't think my personal life was of concern to my employer."

"Not to your employer…to a friend."

She raised a brow. "Now we're friends?"

She was making this hard on him, but he supposed

he couldn't blame her. She must be terribly confused about their relationship by now. "I'd say that two people who strip naked and propose to make love have crossed the outer boundaries of a business relationship."

"True," she allowed. "Go on."

"You were open with me about your past and about your pledge to yourself. I appreciate that, although it came at a rather awkward moment."

"For both of us," she murmured.

"Yes," he quickly agreed. "What I'm trying to say is, I don't think I handled it very well." Moving his chair around from his side of the table to be closer to her, he took her hand in his. "I guess that's because you scared the hell out of me."

"*I* scared *you?*" She looked amazed. "I was terrified I wouldn't live up to your expectations in bed. When you left the room that night, I was sure you were disappointed in me."

"Not disappointed in the way you think." How to explain? "You see, some men look on deflowering virgins as a kind of sport. Others of us view it as a responsibility…a pretty serious one. What happens that first time for a woman can determine how she feels about sex for a very long time, perhaps even for the rest of her life. It's a lot for any man to take on."

She blinked at him. "I never thought of it that way."

"I nearly ran out of the penthouse that night. I wanted you, but I didn't want the responsibility. And I was angry because I felt you were using me."

"*I* was using *you!*" She stared at him in disbelief.

He nodded. "You'd decided that you no longer wanted to be a virgin. I was the convenient male. I don't like being viewed as a tool."

She muffled a laugh behind her fingertips, then made an effort to face him with a solemn expression. "Sorry. It was just—"

"Poor choice of words. The thing is, I decided that I shouldn't leave you dangling like this. If you are serious about wanting to learn about making love, I'm willing to offer myself as a safe partner."

It must have taken a moment for his meaning to sink in, because her eyes didn't focus on him for several seconds. "You're kidding, right?"

He shook his head and didn't smile even a little bit.

"I—I don't know what to say." Her eyes glittered as if close to tears, before sharpening to bright points and fixing on him with sudden alertness. "If this is your way of poking fun at me, I don't find it amusing."

"Not poking fun." He touched a finger to the tip of her nose and smiled. "Wouldn't do that to you."

She fidgeted on her chair, looking pensively toward a distant island.

"Listen, Abby," Matt continued, "I won't pretend that making love to you will be a chore. I'm very attracted to you. You already know that. You're a very special woman, and I want you as much as, I believe, you want me. But if we do this, if we follow our instincts and become intimate, I'll be making a substantial sacrifice."

She frowned prettily, and more than anything he wanted to kiss her then and there. "I don't understand," she murmured.

"Our professional relationship will change, probably for the worse. It might end completely because of the strong emotional issues involved." Her eyes grew wide as he lifted her fingertips to his lips and brushed them lightly. Her answering shiver vibrated through his own body. "I will probably lose the most effective hostess I've ever had, and that's no small thing to me."

"Your offer..." She ran the tip of her tongue nervously over her upper lip. "I want to take you up on your offer. *I do.*" Her eyes shone eagerly, but something was holding her back. He listened hard to her next words. "I can't afford to be without a job if this suddenly turns sour and we find it impossible to work together."

He let out a long, held breath. If that was all that was bothering her... "Already taken care of," he said with a smile.

"Oh?"

"Your contract. It states that you are guaranteed at least a full year's work, or severance pay to cover the same."

"You mean, you can't fire me for a whole year?"

"You get paid even if you quit tomorrow. Enough security for you, Abby?"

She nodded. "That's more than fair." He noticed a subtle trembling in her hands as they lay on the table.

"One night, if that's all you want. I won't press you for more."

She gave a grim little smirk. "No strings. Isn't that the perfect sexual encounter from the male perspective?"

"Not always," he said softly. "I want you to be sure. Really sure that this is what you want." He touched her cheek gently. "This isn't about me, for once. It's whatever is right for you. Take some time to think about it.''

She smiled gratefully up at him. ''Yes...yes, I will.''

That night, as Abby lay in bed, she felt a restlessness she'd never known before. At one time she'd been proud of the control she had over her life. The freedom to reject sex had been liberating. She would decide when and where it would happen for her—and with whom. No man could take that away from her.

Yes, young men had tempted her. Particularly Richard. But not so much that she had trouble telling them no. In her heart, she knew she could never tell Matt that she didn't want him to touch her. Fate, destiny, something more powerful than human will had taken over, and she felt helpless to change what must be.

Abby pulled the sheets up to her chin and stared wide-eyed at the white ceiling and the slowly turning fan. As if he were in the room with her, she could feel Matt's hands gliding over her body, soothing and exciting her all in the same moment. Her heart was racing, although she lay absolutely still. She wanted him desperately.

# Six

Bristol Cove was an intimate pink-sand beach on the south shore of Paget Parish. Unlike the famous Elbow Beach or Horseshoe Bay, which attracted large numbers of tourists in season, the secluded cove was visited mostly by locals and often remained completely deserted. "I discovered this place a few years ago," Matt explained the next day as he helped Abby down the steps cut into the limestone cliff.

The path was narrow, edged in blooming shrubs. The arms of the cove closed in an embrace, sheltering the beach, keeping the water calm, offering a haven for the colorful little fish that darted in and out of the submerged coral reef.

Abby wished she were one of those little fish, hiding in among the lovely branches of coral. The simple fact that she and Matt had discussed sleeping together had set her on pins and needles. Could she actually do what Matt proposed and she had assured him she wanted to do? Could she simply have sex with him as an educational experience, then return to business as usual?

He had made no promise of a future for them; he'd implied much the opposite. But she'd approached this same point in her life once before, with Richard, and later wondered if she'd done the right thing by turning him away. She cared more about Matt, surprisingly, than she had ever cared about the man she had promised to marry. Now she wondered if she ever let Matt possess her body would she be letting him take her heart, too? And once that happened, would she find the strength to walk away from him when the time came?

Shivering despite the warm tropical breeze off the water, she followed Matt onto the pale crescent of sand. "This is the most beautiful place I've ever seen," she whispered.

"It's a favorite of mine," he admitted, dropping towels onto the sand. "There are others that come to mind, though."

"Where?"

"Castle Donan. Haven't been there in years, but it's a breathtaking estate. You should travel to Scotland someday. You'd love it."

She smiled at the fantasy. Did he really think she would ever have that kind of money? He must, having said it so casually.

"Then there's Elbia, just the other side of the mountains from Austria," he added. "That's where my other brother and his wife live."

"Another castle?"

He chuckled at the skepticism in her voice. "Believe it or not, yes. But only one good-sized private suite belongs to Thomas. I think I mentioned that he's employed by King Jacob. The mountains there are amazing. You feel as if you're ten miles in the sky."

Abby let out a long breath. "Your family sounds pretty amazing." She nibbled at her lower lip. "You must miss them."

He shrugged, but the gesture was anything but casual.

"How long has it been since you've seen your father?" She waited for a response, but none came. Perhaps she shouldn't have brought up the subject.

Instead of answering her, Matt faced the water, pulled his shirt off over his head and marched with purpose toward the turquoise wavelets. Forbidden topic. She decided to give him some space to work out whatever was bothering him.

Abby flipped a towel flat on the sand and stretched out on it. The sun was warm and yellow above her. Its heat toasted her skin pleasantly. She had smoothed on sunblock back at the house and wouldn't worry about burning. Wedging her hands beneath her chin, she watched Matt dive into the waste-deep water and swim away from her. The muscles across his shoulder blades kneaded and stretched with each stroke. Her stomach did a funny little dance in appreciation of his fine male physique.

She smiled. This was nice. No pressure to make a decision yet. No need to do anything but laze in the sun. She let her eyes drift closed.

"Time for a swim," a voice from above stated.

"Uh-uh," she grunted contentedly, not bothering to open her eyes. "I'm perfectly happy right here."

"Last warning. It's in the water or else." His no-

nonsense tone told her she'd better pay attention. She rolled over and squinted up at him. Matt was standing over her, a child's plastic bucket dripping water.

"You wouldn't," she challenged him. After all, he wouldn't drench their towels, would he?

"Try me, lady."

She stuck her tongue out at him.

He tipped the bucket.

Abby squealed and braced herself for the cold splash. But the water was a pleasant lukewarm and actually felt good after the sun's heat. Nevertheless, she leaped up and gave chase, as that was one of the time-honored rules for beach play. Matt dropped the bucket and lit out for the water.

"You'll pay, Lord Smythe!" she shouted, feeling like a teenager again.

"Have to catch me first!" He dove beneath the mirror of blue water.

Beneath the surface, Abby could see his body cutting through the shimmering liquid. Then he was gone...without a trace. She looked around in astonishment, growing worried when he didn't pop up in any of the places she thought he might. The first clue that she'd been duped came at the moment she felt both of her ankles being grasped. Her feet were pulled out from under her. Down she went.

Abby resurfaced, sputtering, laughing and shrieking at Matt in mock indignation. "You scared me to death!"

"Good." He shook the water out of his eyes and grinned wolfishly at her. "Meant to."

"Why?"

"So you'd cling to me for safety."

She laughed. "Fat chance."

He lifted a dark brow. "When I was under, I saw a sand shark."

Abby threw her arms around his neck and drew her feet up to her chest. "Out! Get me out of here this minute."

He was laughing at her. "It was just a baby, harmless. Come on, let's go back for the masks and fins. I want to show you my pets."

She scowled at him as he slid an arm under her knees and started carrying her toward shore. "If your pets are larger than a bread box and have teeth, forget it."

He grinned. "You'll love them."

A few minutes later, they were back in the water, and Abby was enjoying the ease and speed of swimming with big blue flippers on her feet. Although she wasn't a strong swimmer, she had no trouble keeping up with Matt as they kicked toward the reef. She dipped her face into the warm water as they neared the coral outcroppings that sheltered the cove, and breathed through the snorkel.

The water was clear and she could see bright flashes of color flitting here and there ahead of them. Matt pointed out and named them for her. Blue and yellow butterfly fish. Black with white angel fish. Silvery needle fish almost as clear as the water. Comical Sergeant Majors, so curious they swam right up to her mask.

She lifted her head and treaded water while pushing the breathing tube from her mouth. "Your pets?"

Matt lifted his mask. "Mine and everyone else's. There are dozens of species living in the waters around Bermuda."

"They're so bright, they don't look real," Abby

said. She replaced her mask and swam a little farther, fascinated by the graceful little creatures. This was a dreamworld she never wanted to leave.

They swam for another hour. Eventually her legs began to feel wobbly, and hunger made land look appealing again.

"Had enough?" Matt asked softly. There were underlying meanings in his tone. She looked away, unable to meet his dark eyes.

"For now," she said. "Can we come back in after lunch?"

"If you like." He took her hand in his as they swam back toward the beach. When they were in shallow enough water to stand, she put her feet down in the soft sand. The water lapped delightfully around her, lifting her breasts with each subtle undulation.

Matt stopped in front of her. "You seemed to enjoy yourself." He pulled off his mask and snorkel then tossed them along with Abby's and the rest of their equipment up onto the sand.

"I loved it." Abby's eyes sparkled up at him. "Thank you."

He couldn't imagine why he hadn't thought her the most beautiful woman on earth the first moment he'd set eyes on her. Without makeup, her hair slicked back from her face, droplets clinging to her eyelashes—she was no less than perfect.

He had no alternative but to kiss her. Moving his free hand quickly behind her neck, he brought her forward to meet him. He kissed her deeply, savoring the taste of the sea on her lips. He was lost.

In the next seconds, only scattered thoughts registered in his mind. The beach was deserted but for them. He moved her a few feet farther away from

shore, into deeper water. Her eyes widened question-
ingly but showed no fear. Good, he thought, if she'd
been afraid of him, he would have had to stop.

He only meant to play…just a little bit, for a short
while. To kiss. To touch beneath the water. To give
her a brief preview of the sensations she might look
forward to when…*if* they slept together. He didn't
think of what he was doing as seduction until his hand
slipped beneath the warm water, touched her breast
and felt the nipple harden and raise beneath his
thumb. She looped her arms up and around his neck,
and he eased her closer, then still closer until their
bodies pressed one against the other. Matt felt himself
swell and grow rigid against the flat of her belly. He
looked down into her eyes and saw that she had felt
it, too. She didn't pull away.

"Pretty easy to see where my thoughts are," he
whispered.

She nodded, dreamy-eyed in the shoulder-deep water.

"But I'm not going to make love to you here. Not
now."

"Why not?"

"You need more time to consider what you're giving away."

"I'm more concerned about what I might lose,"
she murmured. "And I don't mean my virginity."

"What about that husband in the future? He'll
know."

"Maybe he'll have to accept me as I am."

As she was. Beautiful. Abby was pure joy to look
upon, to be with. She made him feel all male. She
dragged him out of his world of business deals, competition with himself and with others, even out of the

pain of the past. He could see need in her eyes, desire, and he wanted more than anything to give her the pleasure she so longed for.

Yet, did he dare take from her the one treasure she'd safeguarded all of her life? She claimed she was ready. But could he believe her?

If only there was a way to…

He smiled at the unexpected thought. Why not?

"Watch for intruders," he said huskily. Before she could ask why, he ducked beneath the water, pushed her swimming suit top up over her breasts and closed his lips around one nipple. He felt her tense, then wiggle with pleasure as she clamped her hands on either side of his head beneath the water. He suckled her as long as his breath held out, then broke the surface to gasp for air.

"Oh, Matt. Oh…" She was panting and smiling and laughing out loud, as ready as any woman he'd ever known. But he still cautioned himself to give her only as much as she could handle. Or maybe it was more a question of how much he could handle without losing control of his own body. Her pleasure alone must be all that mattered, for now.

He leaned down and kissed her on the mouth, and she opened her lips to allow him to touch his tongue to hers. He let his hands follow the lines of her body, beneath the water. Kittenish sounds of frustrated delight escaped from her lips. With one hand he cupped her bottom and caressed her softly. The other moved between their bodies, stroking the inside of her thigh, sliding upward, finding the elastic opening of her bathing suit leg.

He waited, letting her get used to the touch of his hand, giving her time to react—to push him away, show any sign of fear or uneasiness. But she was returning his kisses with fervor now. Smoothing her palms up over his bare chest, she curled her fingers between spirals of dark hair.

When she pressed herself against his hand cupped between her thighs, he took that for as green a light as he was likely to get. Matt slid his fingers inside the stretchy fabric and found the fragile lips of her womanhood. If he touched her just right, *there...* If he didn't give into the impulse to penetrate her, he'd do no physical damage.

His fingertips moved in slow, gentle circles, pressing upward against the moist, velvety flesh, but not forcing within her. Abby began to respond in an instinctive rhythm to his touch. Her head fell back and her eyes closed. Her face shone as brightly as a new day's sun. Her eyelashes fluttered, her lips pouted, drew inward, then parted. The elegant contours of her face displayed a hundred subtle emotions. He loved watching her.

"Tell me if you're not all right," he whispered in her ear.

She didn't respond, and he wondered if she had even heard him. He sensed that she was concentrating very hard on the touch of his hands, the feelings rushing through her. Cradling her against him, he slowly, patiently moved a single wide finger over the velvety nubbin, flicking it again and again. Until she shuddered and clutched at his shoulders, her fingernails digging into his flesh.

At last he felt her body go rigid then convulse on waves of pleasure so intense he could only imagine. Abby buried her face in his chest and smothered ecstatic whimpers he felt as vibrations through his entire body.

Matt continued to hold her, supporting her in the water while her world steadied, her legs found their strength again and her breathing evened out. He grinned. Not a bad compromise at that. He had kept the woman's virtue intact, at least in the anatomical sense, while showing her what all the excitement was about. Lesson #1.

Only problem was—he ached for her. Never before had he been so moved by witnessing a woman's passion. She aroused his own need to the very edge of the male precipice…but he wouldn't ask her to satisfy him. That would have to wait, although waiting was a gamble. What if she changed her mind about wanting Lesson #2?

Matt started to walk them toward the beach, his arm low around Abby's waist, guiding her unsteady steps through the water. She brought him to a halt. "Not yet," she whispered throatily, and looked up at him with a far different expression than he'd ever seen in those coffee-and-cream eyes.

He chuckled. "Don't tell me you want more?"

"Yes." She blinked up at him. "But not for myself."

He stared down at her in disbelief. "We agreed to wait for the rest, until you had time to think."

She shrugged, a soft smile lifting her moist lips. "I was just considering alternatives. You did that to me. You made me…made my body feel wonderful things." She shook her head in amazement, unable to find words to explain what had just happened to her. "What is that called?"

He laughed. "Let's just say I was making love to you with my hands."

"I had no idea. I thought there had to be…thought you needed to—" She blushed and looked away from him.

"So now you know." But she still wouldn't allow him to move toward the shore. She took a hasty look around.

"No one saw," he assured her.

"I know," she said, then smiled impishly at him. "It wasn't that."

"What then?"

"A woman can do something similar for a man, am I right?"

"Well, yes…" Abby must have seen movies, read books. The act of sex was less a mystery these days to the uninitiated. "But you don't need to—"

She straightened her shoulders, lifted her chin and faced him with an adorably solemn expression. Then he felt her small hand press over him through the fabric of his trunks. Matt flinched, then locked his knees and let her satisfy her curiosity.

"You're very, um…taut," she announced.

"Yes." He stifled a laugh. He was a steel rod, for all the good it was going to do. A cold shower, a short brandy…he'd survive.

"Does it hurt?" she asked curiously.

"Difficult to explain. I'm not in actual pain."

"But you'd feel better if—" She let the twinkle in her eyes finish the message.

"Come on, we'd better go," he growled. His will-power was seeping away with every minute he lingered in the warm water with her. Didn't she know the hell she was putting him through? Making him stand here with her, after having touched her that way, after having felt her release herself to him.

"In a minute," she said firmly.

Her fingers slipped into his trunks and wrapped around him. He let out a groan and looked hastily around. No one on the beach. No one on the cliffs above. All the action was beneath the waterline anyway.

Abby moved her hand experimentally along him, her fingers gently encircling him. "Tell me what to do," she whispered.

Matt shut his eyes to better absorb the pleasure she was bringing him. "Woman, you're doing it."

She stroked him until his body pulsed with fire. Burying his face in the damp waves on top of her head, he bit down hard on his lower lip to stop himself from bellowing out her name. Flames roared through him. He pressed against her hand and let nature take its glorious course.

For a considerable while, the world went away.

He couldn't tell how many minutes passed. But when he opened his eyes she was standing back from him, her arms lapped around his hips, watching him. "Thanks," he murmured dryly and lifted her hand to his lips.

"My pleasure." She gave him a smug little smile.

For the first time, he feared he might have unleashed forces far beyond his control.

# Seven

"**I**diot!"

Matt had made a huge mistake. A mistake that was going to cost him more than he could predict even at this moment when thoughts came more clearly to him. How had he ever convinced himself that he could act as sexual mentor to Abby without becoming...becoming what? Becoming *involved* with her. Already he felt addicted to the way a clear golden light shone through her brown eyes when she gazed up at him.

He'd left Abby a note that afternoon saying he had business in Hamilton and would return in time for dinner at La Coquille. But he had no business, he felt he just had to walk somewhere...anywhere. However, what Matt was doing now couldn't be called walking. He ate up ground in long, powerful strides. He moved fast and furiously for a full six miles west of Hamilton, through the country lanes of Pembroke Parish, down narrow paths nearly taken over by tropical growth, along the low cliffs of the north shore, past cottages and through hamlets, until welcome exhaustion overcame him. He stopped to sit on a rock, held his head in his hands and groaned in frustration with himself.

When he had first planned how he might initiate her into the mysteries of womanhood, he had viewed the process as very simple, even mechanical. He had suspected he'd have one hell of a good time teaching her; he wasn't a fool. But he had no warning of how powerful her impact on him would be. Or of the unfamiliar feelings she'd elicit. Protectiveness…desire…possessiveness…and other tender, undefinable feelings he didn't dare analyze too closely.

And now, what was he supposed to do? He had made a pact with her. He had given her a taste of intimacy so intense that even he, the well-initiated to sexual encounters, had been overwhelmed by their coming together. It hadn't mattered that they had stopped short of intercourse in the traditional sense. Everything else they'd done had felt like…like what?

"It wasn't sex," he whispered, amazed by the direction his mind was tumbling, not wanting to believe what he was thinking. "It *was* making love."

But that wasn't the same as being in love. No. You could care about a person and still not be in love with them, he argued silently. Love was a very touchy subject, and something he'd avoided all his life. Love meant fragile attachments, which could be broken even when one didn't want them to break. Love meant committing to one person and trusting that person to honor promises and never leave. His mother had left them. His father had left his sons too, perhaps not physically and not immediately…but he'd absented himself in spirit from his sons. The distance between them had been gaping and unvarying. No warmth, no admission of love. Ever.

And now Abby, little Abby who didn't have a clue what making love was all about, had become a threat to the shield he'd built around himself. The shield called Smythe International. If he had any sense at all, he would keep on walking until he hit the sea, then jump on the first boat for the States. He should keep on going and never look back.

But he had promised Abby certain things. An education in both the import business and the bedroom. Never in his life had he gone back on his word. This had been the sacred rule of his life—to never do to someone else what his parents had done to him.

La Coquille was located, surprisingly, in a marine museum called the Bermuda Underwater Exploration Institute. Nevertheless, it was considered by many to be the best gourmet restaurant on the island. The elegant dining room was white from top to bottom, enclosed by glass and overlooking Hamilton's famous harbor. The waiters were attentive and polite. The atmosphere was one of modern polish and romantic simplicity.

It was difficult for Abby to choose from among the delicacies offered on the menu. She at last opted for just two courses: a cold gazpacho soup served with chunks of fresh lobster, and steamed mussels in a white wine and Pernod cream sauce, with a garlic-rubbed baguette. Matt followed his soup with a huge salad brimming with mesclun leaves, shrimps, avocado, baby artichokes, calamata olives, tiny tomatoes and a walnut oil dressing, and this was in turn followed by a seared rack of lamb with sun-dried tomato crust, whipped potatoes with roasted garlic, and rosemary jus.

Abby ate with relish, chattering between bites, ignoring Matt's unexplained sullenness. She refused to let his mysteriously dark mood spoil what remained of the most remarkable day of her life. When the meal was over and coffee poured, she knew she could wait no longer to give Matt her decision.

She'd spent the afternoon digesting the implications of what had happened in the cove that morning.

At the time, their intimacy had seemed a natural progression of their growing closeness. Genuine affection. Adult play. She didn't know why she felt this way with Matt, which was so different from experiences she'd had with men before. His kisses…the way he'd touched her…the *places* he'd touched her…. All seemed part of a dance for which she'd stood in the wings all of her adult life, waiting to perform. She'd only been lacking the right partner.

When he took her in his arms and the look in his eyes told her that he had plans for her—intimate, secret, delicious plans—she hadn't felt the least trepidation. It had just felt right.

Matt had taught her a lot in the span of a few exhilarating minutes. He had taught her about her own body—its hungers and ways to satisfy them. He had also allowed her a glimpse of her own power to arouse a man, and to gratify him. It thrilled her that she had given Matt pleasure equal to her own. She wanted to repeat their sensual dance, to learn the next step…and the next…until she had mastered all there was to the entire ballet.

"Look," she began slowly, "I don't know what's bothering you. But we can't just not talk about what happened this morning, or about what we are going to do from here on."

Matt drew a deep breath and moved his lips but, at first, nothing came out. "Of course," he finally managed. "Let's not do it here, though. Finish your coffee and we'll take a carriage back to the house. It will give us time to talk."

Several horse-drawn carriages were parked along Front Street, just below the restaurant. Matt arranged a route with the driver. Then he and Abby settled themselves into a seat beneath the pink-fringed canopy. She nestled against his arm as he rested it along the seat back. She felt him tense but did not move away. Neither spoke for several minutes as the horse clop-clopped along the narrow streets between colorful shops. It was Abby who felt she must clear the air or burst.

"At the cove this morning," she began nervously, "you made it so easy to be with you." She drew a deep breath for strength. "And all day long I've thought of nothing but—"

"You don't know what you're saying," he snapped. "What you felt then and still feel now, is called lust. A taste of it, and people do insane things."

Abby considered this. "No," she said slowly, "I don't think it can be just that." Of course, she tingled at the thought of his body reacting to her touch, and her own body responding to his. It was delicious just to remember. But there must have been some other reason why she'd thrown off a lifetime of caution and a solemn vow. "I feel differently about you than any other man I've known."

He paled and looked away.

"Matt," she said angrily, but lowered her voice to keep the driver from hearing, "I'm not so naïve that I expect a lifetime commitment because we were intimate. No one's mentioning the *L* word here. I just want you to know that I've made my decision. I want to sleep with you."

His scowl nearly broke her heart. "That isn't wise," he whispered.

"It was your suggestion!"

"I know, but I was acting…I don't know…selfishly, I suppose. Men say a lot of things to get women into bed."

A chill settled at the back of her spine. Was that all this was? Could any woman have been with him at the cove today and received the same attentions?

She bit her bottom lip and stared into the dark as the whistle of the tree frogs filled the night with music her heart didn't want to hear.

"Listen," he said, his tone softer. "You've waited this long. You'll regret doing this now."

"No," she said firmly. "I know what I want." And *I want you*, Matthew Smythe, the words erupted silently in her head. "Things have changed…*I* have changed. Maybe I don't want to go to my marriage bed without understanding how to please my husband. Maybe I don't want to always wonder if the man I marry will be able to satisfy me," she said under her breath but with an urgency she felt deep down in her soul.

Matt winced. He hated hearing her talk this way. The mere notion of another man touching her, sent him teetering into rage. What had he been doing? Preparing her for another man who would someday reap the benefits of his instruction?

But if she was so set on making the leap from virgin to woman-of-the-world, did he want to pass off that duty to someone else? He was trapped. There was no place of comfort for him. Either way—make love to Abby or not—he would eventually be the loser. He couldn't turn her away, and he couldn't keep her.

"Matt?" He became vaguely aware that she was repeating his name. "Matt, are you all right?" Her hand settled gently over his. "I said, if you have changed your mind and *don't* want to be my lover..."

The disappointment mirrored in her eyes nearly shattered him. "Of course it's not that. I don't want to hurt you, that's all." Not *all*. He didn't want to destroy himself either. But the temptation was just too great. She was beautiful, willing, eager, and the cove had shown him her potential as a generous lover. What man could turn down an offer like that?

The carriage pulled up in front of the house, and Matt paid the driver. He helped Abby down to the pebbly path and held her hand as they walked in silence toward the front door.

With each step, he cursed himself and his runaway libido. He should be strong enough to walk away from her without explanation. He had done it dozens of times with other women—sent flowers and an innocuous note thanking her for a pleasant evening. Never lying, but letting them know that they shouldn't expect to hear from him again.

But Abby...he couldn't do that to her. Something had happened between them since they met, something that connected him to her in a baffling but undeniable way.

He looked around. Somehow they had made it through the door and into the foyer without his realizing it. She was standing in front of him, looking expectantly at him, her eyes wide, welcoming, hopeful.

He shook his head in defeat. "Heaven help me, but I want you."

"I want you too, Matt," she whispered, brushing her lips delicately across his. "What are you afraid of? I'm the one who's supposed to be nervous."

That did him in. His masculine pride seized him by the scruff of his neck and hauled him out of inaction. "I'm not afraid!" He glared down at her. "I'm just trying to be a gentleman about this...this mess you've gotten us into."

"Mess?" She pouted at him.

He supposed she was taunting him now, challenging him not to back out of their deal. Even knowing what she was doing, he couldn't stop himself from reacting to the pretty flush of color in her cheeks and playful sparkle in her eyes. He took a step forward and enfolded her in his arms.

"You're in for it now, woman," he growled.

She accepted his kiss and gave back to him as much ardor. Picking her up in his arms, he carried her swiftly up the steps to his bedroom, taking the steps in twos, thankful the staff had left for the night.

He didn't want hushed, quick, mechanical sex. He wanted to spend an entire night with Abigail Benton, relearning the art of making love as she experienced it for the first time. He wanted to gentle her, then ravish her. He wanted to see sweet shock then drowsy pleasure in her eyes. He wanted to hear her cry out his name, while he howled like a wild creature at mating.

It had been a long time since he'd wanted a woman more than once in a night. He knew he'd take Abby as many times as she let him, or until he sensed her body's exhaustion.

Matt kicked open the bedroom door and crossed the room in two eager strides. Although he'd meant to lay her gently on the bed, he was so excited he dropped her from two feet above the mattress. "Sorry."

She bounced, laughing up at him. "Is that what they call foreplay? Battering the female?"

He grinned wolfishly as he unclasped his belt. "Very funny. Take off your clothes, woman."

"No." She tilted her head and looked up at him impishly. "You do it."

*Someone help me!* he thought desperately. *I won't last five minutes.*

He cautioned himself to move slowly, remember how new all of this was to her. No matter how urgently he wanted her, or how ready he was for her, he must be responsible for causing her as little pain and as much pleasure as possible. A delicate balance to strike.

He tossed his belt onto a chair. His shirt followed. She was wearing a blue dress that zipped up the back. The skirt was full, lying in ripples above her knees now. He sat on the edge of the bed, took one of her stockinged feet in his hands and stroked the curve of her instep. His mind was spinning, his body throbbing, but he forced himself to move slowly, starting as far away from where he wanted to end up, to give

himself time to calm down and slowly bring her up
to meet his state of readiness.

There was something else new about this experience, he suddenly realized. He'd never been with a
woman who hadn't already slept with other men. He
knew what he was supposed to find, anatomically, and
vaguely what would occur when he entered her. But
how to choreograph the important moment, he didn't
have a clue. In this way, he was as inexperienced as
she was.

His hands worked slowly but with a purpose. As
she sat on the bed watching him, he smoothed his
fingers around her instep, over her slim ankle, and
upwards along her calf. "Take them off," he whispered, indicating her pantyhose.

She slid off the beige hose and let them fall beside
the bed, her eyes wider now, with a touch of appre-
hension. He caressed one long, silky limb, raised her
foot then grinned at her over it.

She lifted a questioning brow and mouthed, *What?*

He liked that this was all surprises for her. Feeling
devilish, he brought her toes to his lips and kissed
each of them. She shivered, giving an extra little
quiver like a kitten waking from a nap. Her smile was
curious, serene and eager all at the same time. He
drew the tip of his tongue up the sole of her foot; she
tasted of baby powder and vanilla.

Letting out a little whimper, she curled her toes.

"All right?" he asked.

"Yes…definitely, yes," she squeaked.

Delighting in her reaction, he pressed out a row of
soft kisses around her instep to the top of her foot,
her ankle, and up over her knee and thigh. More than
anything at that moment, he wanted to continue along

the silky path of flesh and taste her essence. But it was much too soon for that. He feared she might be frightened or panic, then he would have failed at his task. He promised himself that treat later, if she allowed him.

His hands worked with expert ease now, moving behind her back to unzip her dress, sliding her delicate shoulders free, unhooking her bra, letting her dress and panties disappear over the edge of the bed. At last, he had her naked before him.

Matt didn't want to make her feel self-conscious, but he couldn't help sitting back for a moment to study her. He let his hands travel over her body, memorizing her as a blind man learns a person's face by touch. Her breasts were small, tight and deliciously budded with small brown nipples. Her waist was slim but not emaciated or hardened with unnatural muscle. Her hips…ah, her hips beckoned to him and he cupped her bottom with his hands. She lifted her knees, opening herself to him.

"Abby," he breathed, "do you have any idea how beautiful you are?"

She smiled indulgently up at him, looking not at all afraid. "Bet you say that to all the girls."

He had to some. This time he meant it.

"All those years, you must have had to fight the boys off with a club."

She grinned. "No clubs handy tonight."

"I can see that," he whispered hoarsely. "Listen, if I do anything that hurts you, tell me. If I don't react fast enough, slug me. I have a feeling I might get carried away, and I don't want you to think you have to submit to something that you don't feel comfortable doing."

"All right," Abby agreed solemnly. She looked down. "You have a beautiful chest." She touched him lightly, still unsure why she felt not a lick of fear or timidity. She had imagined being overcome by the awkwardness of the moment. She had been sure she would feel embarrassed, vulnerable, even terrified when lying naked before a man. None of that even entered her mind. She let her fingertips drift through the short curls over his muscled chest, then let them trail down his stomach to his hips. "Do those come off?"

He followed her gaze to his pants. "Occasionally."

She thought she noticed a slight trembling in his fingers as he unzipped then stood beside the bed to step out of them. Before he could remove the black briefs he wore underneath, she reached up and drew one finger along the diagonal ridge outlined by the fabric. It felt firm and interesting.

He smiled at her, grasped her hand and pressed her palm over him. "That means the man behind the weapon finds you very appealing, miss."

"Learn something new every day."

"Ready for more?"

She nodded.

He edged the wide elastic band down over his hips, then all the way off. She fixed a wide-eyed look on him, ran her tongue between her lips twice, and swallowed. "Oh my…"

He laughed at her expression, one of mixed disbelief and intrigue. "Like what you see?"

"I…well, of course I…" She gazed helplessly up at him. "I'm afraid I'm too small. I mean just look at you…I could never—"

"You will," he said with quiet certainty. "Move over, Abby."

She slid to one side, keeping him in sight, watching for sudden moves. The one thing she didn't want to do was scream or react foolishly to something that would be natural to an experienced woman, because then he wouldn't make love to her. More than anything at this moment, she longed for that.

He stretched out beside her. "I'll take it easy. Promise."

She nodded.

"Remember the cove?"

She felt a heady warmth rise within her, intensified by their nakedness. "Yes," she whispered.

"May I touch you like I did there?"

"Umm-hmm."

She watched his eyes, his wonderful dark eyes as his hand lowered beneath her sight line. Then she felt his fingertips moving between her thighs. She let her knees fall a little farther apart.

"Relaxed?" he asked.

"Oh sure," she said. "Like a cat in a clothes dryer."

He chuckled. His hand rested over the softly furred mound of her womanhood, moving in soothing circles. His head lowered, until his mouth closed over her breast. She felt all the tension drain from her body as his tongue and teeth played with her nipple, drawing her into his mouth.

"Better," she murmured. "Oh, that's nice, too."

His hand was finding the same spot it had found at the cove, a sensitive little button of flesh between her legs. Each time his finger flicked over it, her heart

fluttered, her insides tightened, and a flash of heat
burst through her.

He was slipping his finger a little deeper each time
it came back to center…a little deeper…a little
firmer…a little more persistent. She stared up into his
eyes. They were kind, concerned and observant of
every nuance of emotion in her features. For a second,
his hand seemed to falter, as if he wasn't sure of
himself.

She quickly grabbed his wrist. "Please…don't
stop, Matt. I won't change my mind."

With a nod he slipped his finger just a fraction of
an inch into her. It felt tight but not painful. "Just
another minute," he leaned down to whisper into her
ear then stayed low over her. "Hold on to me."

She gripped his shoulders, and felt a second finger
press close to the first, then move against the tight-
ness. There was a bright burst of sensation that moved
so quickly past discomfort it didn't seem important.
Slowly, with great gentleness, Matt moved his fingers
within her, bringing lovely, healing warmth, tingles
of a sort she'd never felt before, waves of pleasure so
brilliant and potent she could only hold on to his muscled shoulders, now glistening with sweat, and let him
lift her higher into a place she'd never been.

She was so swept away by the feelings he was
bringing to her, she hardly was aware of his moving
momentarily to reach for protection. Then she felt him
shift his weight above her, bring himself between her
thighs, and enter the swollen, moist passage. It became a new dance. With a feeling that her partner had
fully mastered each step. And they rose and fell together until the room spun and her body felt as if it

were consumed by flames. At last Matt lifted himself above her and groaned with primal satisfaction, arching his back and pressing fully within her. He had been right. He fit. All of him. Much to her delight.

# Eight

$M$att woke and it was still dark outside. He turned his head to look at Abby, hugging a pillow, turned on her side away from him. Reaching over he lifted a strand of hair covering her eyes. She sighed softly.

"Come," he whispered. "Come to me."

She shifted sleepily, moving as if in a dream, shoving the pillow away and rolling toward him, her eyes still closed. Her cheek rested on his chest, her right leg hooked over his hip. Closing his arms around her protectively, he knew that nothing about this night could be bad. She had been perfect, and he had only faltered that once when he suddenly feared letting her down.

The doubts that had plagued him earlier in the evening were miraculously gone. Nothing much seemed to matter except being close to Abby. And two people couldn't get much closer. Her skin felt flushed, alive, soft against the muscle and sinew of his body. The image of flesh on flesh drew itself out, tempting him again.

"You awake, Ab?" he whispered, feeling the urge again, needing to feed his hunger for her. They had already made love twice. Once because there had been work to be done. The second time because she had asked, shyly but with a serious gleam in her eyes he found charming and irresistible. He had enthusiastically obliged.

"Sleeping," she murmured. The corners of her lips turned up. "Go away."

"Lots of time for laziness tomorrow." He gently rolled her to her other side, tucking her bottom against him as he moved onto his side. Slipping his arms around her from behind, he buried his face in her whisper-soft hair and fondled her breasts until he sensed from her pleased wriggles that she was fully awake and eager for another lesson.

"Something new?" she asked breathily.

"If you like."

She turned her head against the pillow, looking back over her shoulder at him and stretched up to kiss the underside of his whiskery chin. "I like." Her voice was trusting, eager, and happy—and worked like magic on his body. He felt full against her plush little bottom. When he moved within the familiar moist feminine cove, she pressed back against him and reached her climax so quickly he didn't have to wait for his own.

The days that followed spun themselves out like pink cotton candy for Abby. During the past three weeks, they'd spent long hours in bed, touching each other, talking, laughing, making love. She learned ways to arouse him almost instantly. She discovered the few places he didn't like to be touched and many more he did. Before they had become intimate, nearly all they talked about and nearly all Matt did was involved in Smythe International. Now he avoided mention of business. All he wanted to do was talk about her, about them, about the music of the happy little tree frogs and which flowers had bloomed in the garden that day.

"My favorites are the hibiscus," Abby said with a sigh. "The ultimate tropical flower—fiery orange, blazing red. Huge, plump blooms and tongues of gold."

"They sacrifice long lives for drama," he murmured, stroking her hair. "Did you know that each blossom lasts only one day?"

She looked up at him from where she lay against his chest. "Really?"

"Really. That's all the time they have."

"How sad." She twirled a finger through short hairs in the center of his stomach. She was about to say that people were like that, sometimes. Some living long, unremarkable lives, while others lit up the world with a brief blaze of glory. Then there were relationships. Some were strong and lasting, but to the observer might seem unexciting. Other couples loved with explosive passion that didn't last.

Was that what she and Matt were? Participants in a brief affair? One-day bloomers?

The ringing of the telephone interrupted thoughts that had become suddenly troubling.

"I'll get it," she said, glad for something to distract her.

"Let me know if it's anything important. We should get up and go outside sometime today." He winked at her in passing on his way into the bathroom.

Abby heard the shower turn on as she picked up the phone.

It was Paula, calling from Chicago. "For days and days I've left messages," she complained as soon as she heard a live voice.

Abby smiled secretively. "Sorry. Things have been busy here."

"I swear, that man can make work for himself even in paradise. Is he eating? Is he getting any sleep?"

She sounded like a typical mother, worrying over her college-age son.

"His appetite is just fine." Abby had to stop herself from adding: And he's eating well, too. A long band of silence came to Abby across the line. "Paula, you still there?"

"Sweet Lord in Heaven, save us all."

"What?"

"He's seduced you, hasn't he?" the older woman groaned. "I'll kill him."

"Now, Paula," Abby said soothingly. "Don't be upset. He's being perfectly wonderful."

"You don't know him like I do. When he's being perfectly wonderful, he's a danger to the entire female gender."

"Believe me, he hasn't taken advantage of me."

"He wouldn't mean to," Paula insisted. "He never means any harm. But he'll hit the wall and it will all get too personal for him. He can't handle forever, darling. He'll break it off as soon as things get serious." She lowered her voice as if she feared, all the way from Chicago, her voice might be heard by her employer. "He tell you about his parents?"

Abby straightened defensively. "Yes."

"Matthew won't risk being left behind again."

Abby wanted to explain that there were no expectations on either side. She wanted to tell Paula that all Matt was doing was guiding her through a challenging time in her life. He was the teacher, she the student. Along the way, he was bringing her immense joy.

But she knew in her heart that she'd stopped thinking about their arrangement in such simple terms. A telling silence stretched between the two women.

At last, Paula's voice came again. "It's too late, isn't it? You've fallen in love with him."

Abby let out a brittle laugh. "That's ridiculous."

Barely a heartbeat passed before Paula murmured, "Abigail, I'm so sorry."

Abby closed her eyes and clutched the receiver. Was it that obvious? "I'll be all right. Really."

"The best thing you can do is get out while you can, dear. I don't want to lose you. I like working with you. But it's going to be hell for you, seeing him every day after it's been like this between the two of you."

"Maybe he won't run this time," Abby said weakly.

"Maybe he'll chuck being an entrepreneur and take up knitting." There was a rustling sound from the other end, as if Paula was shuffling papers. "He works like a maniac for a reason. It's his way of shutting down his emotions. He can't deal with loving a woman. He told me, once, he could still remember his mother's face. He remembers her kissing him goodbye then picking up a suitcase and walking away from him and his brothers.''

"But I'd never leave him," Abby protested. "Not if he wanted me to stay. I'd never hurt him.''

"Are you sure?" Paula asked gently. "What if someone from your past came back into your life?''

Abby frowned. "I don't understand.''

"A man called yesterday. Left a message for you to call him. A Mr. Wooten?''

Abby gasped. "Richard?" The last time she'd seen her fiancé, he had been walking out of her life, with energy. *I can't take the chance of marrying a frigid woman.*

For the first time since they'd broken up, the mention of his name didn't wrench her heart out of her chest. She felt nothing. Another man possessed her, heart and soul. She was in love with Matt.

"Did you tell him I was out of the country?''

"I did, but he was insistent. Said he was your fiancé.''

"Not anymore he isn't," she stated briskly. "That was finished more than a year ago.''

"Maybe not for him.''

Now that was a disturbing thought. "What he wants no longer matters," Abby said.

"Well, don't say I didn't warn you. I told the man you'd call him when you could, but do as you like. Now, I need to talk to that *wonderful* boss of ours.'' Her sarcasm wasn't subtle.

"He's in the shower now," Abby said, feeling a twinge of discomfort at the intimacy of the statement. "I'll have him call you back as soon as he's out.''

She hung up, then stood watching the phone for several minutes, as if she expected it to leap up and bite her. Until this moment, she hadn't admitted to herself, much less to anyone else, that she was in love with Lord Matthew Smythe, the earl of Brighton, president of a multimillion-dollar company. Until this moment, she hadn't acknowledged how quickly and completely she'd become sucked into his world. Or how much of her heart he occupied. To think of sleeping in a bed alone, without Matt beside her, seemed unbearable. To consider sitting down to a table for breakfast without first pouring him a cup of coffee, felt somehow illogical. To forget his touch on her body would be tragic.

She was in deep trouble.

Matt felt free of the world. It was a strange and new sensation. He simply didn't care about anything except being with Abby, he realized as he stood in the shower.

Each day, they had chosen one of a dozen remote coves ringing the island. They held hands, swam and kissed. They'd taken a glass-bottom boat cruise and marveled at the silvery grunts and blue parrot fish skittering in and out of the reefs. Each evening, he'd dismissed his staff early. They dined alone on the veranda in the moonlight, then made love in the high-walled garden amidst the intoxicating perfume of bougainvillea, hibiscus, and delicate purple Bermudiana blossoms.

She was all he longed for in those days.

For once in his life, he wanted to play. He fought being pulled back into the hectic business world and did not return Paula's calls.

When Matt's guests had arrived at the end of the first week, he'd been forced to let them into the world

he and Abby shared. He'd gone through the gracious
motions of entertaining. But across the room, glances
were exchanged, desire grew. When he was at last
alone with Abby, he'd flung himself at her hungrily,
taking her with fierce possessiveness.

Now his thoughts were abruptly ended by the
sound of Abby's voice.

"Paula says it's an emergency, Matt. You really do
have to talk to her."

He grumbled and kissed Abby on the smooth curve
of her throat as he took the receiver from her.
"There's nothing that can't wait until we get back to
Chicago," he barked into the phone.

"Wrong," Paula snapped. "Joseph Cooper has sto-
len two of your best clients. I've been trying to tell
you they wanted to speak with you personally before
turning over their American accounts to him. But
when you stayed in hiding, they were offended. It
looks as if they're going to break their contracts with
us."

He scowled into space, feeling the old aggressiveness begin to seep back into his veins. "Is that so?"

"I'm glad you're taking some time to…" Paula
hesitated. "…to relax. But if you don't come back
soon, Matthew, you may not have a company to come
back to."

He hung up, feeling numb and unsure of himself.
He looked at Abby.

"What's wrong?" she asked softly.

"Time to go back to the real world." Even as he
said the words, he sensed a subtle change in his mind-
set. The real world was in Chicago. Bermuda had
been a kind of fantasy, hadn't it? Here, nothing mattered except making love with a beautiful woman,

watching her smile, listening to her laugh, taking her into his arms each night. Real life wasn't that easy, or pleasant.

Abby studied his expression then gave him a wary smile. "I love this place. Will we be able to come back soon?"

He wasn't sure whether she was talking about Bermuda, or the intimacy they'd shared. Weren't they one and the same? He wondered if it was possible to take what they had found together back into the life he'd known before she walked into it. Sadly, he thought it unlikely.

"We'll see," he murmured, turning away. Outside the window, sailboats drifted across an aquamarine cove. The sky was that vivid, almost surreal blue he had seen only above tropical islands. "Better pack."

The flight back to New York was cloaked in tension. If Abby hadn't known better she would have said that the man sitting beside her on the jet was a stranger. They spoke only a few words during the flight to New York, then transferred to a plane destined for O'Hare. They arrived a little after 8:00 p.m. that same night. A few thousand miles of traveling seemed to have transported her light years away from the man who had made love to her amid lush flowers and the whistling of the tree frogs.

By the time the limo picked them up at the airport, Abby was feeling nauseous, her head throbbed, and she carried with her a sense of deep loss.

"Can you be at the office by nine tomorrow morning?" Matt asked when the car rolled up in front of her apartment.

She turned on the seat to stare at him in disbelief.

"What?" he asked.

The driver came around to open the door for her. She ignored him. "What are we doing, Matt?"

He frowned. "I don't understand." But she could see a nervous glint of recognition in his eyes as he carefully directed them away from hers.

She persisted. "I'm still the same person I was this morning in Bermuda. You are, too." She leaned closer to him, an urgent pressure building in her chest. "I know you're a dedicated workaholic, but what happens to us now? We have to talk."

"This isn't the time." He made a show of consulting his watch. "I have fences to mend, if it isn't already too late."

She understood he was upset to be losing clients. But she suddenly felt left out, and her hurt turned to anger. Tugging the door out of the driver's hand, she slammed it closed, shutting herself inside the limo with Matt. "I believed the lessons ended the first night we made love. After that, everything between us happened because we shared the same affection for each other." Tears clogged her throat, making it far too difficult to speak.

Matt's features hardened. When he at last turned back to her, she couldn't bear the silent message his eyes sent: *We both knew it wasn't going to last.* Overcome with disappointment, Abby slid out of the car and ran for the door to her apartment house. The chauffeur followed with her luggage and insisted on bringing it up to her apartment.

She barely managed to shut the door behind him before she lost control. Why had she made such a fool of herself? The tender glances, passionate touches, shared laughter and intimate embraces—they had meant nothing to him. But to her they had been a beautiful promise.

Abby threw herself onto her bed and wept her heart out. She was grateful Dee was out for the night. She couldn't have tolerated anyone seeing her in this condition.

By morning's first light Abby had cried herself out. She sat up in bed, blew her nose, and reviewed her situation with a clear mind.

She had two immediate choices. She could either admit her fragility and resign from the ideal job. Or she must somehow find the strength to face Matt every day as they worked together.

She washed away the salty tear tracks from her cheeks with cool water, brewed herself a tall mug of dark-roasted coffee, did a load of laundry. By the time she was dressed in business clothes, she was ready to go head-to-head with her boss. She wasn't going to let any man destroy her—not a runaway fiancé, not a playboy aristocrat. To hell with them all!

# Nine

Matt dreaded the next morning. The way he'd treated Abby the night before was inexcusable; but he would have to face her today.

He hadn't meant to hurt her, hadn't stopped to think during those miraculous weeks in Bermuda that it had been more than just having fun to her. He was her first, and that was bound to be special for a woman like Abby. She had cherished her body, saving herself for one special man. He had used her. He *knew* he was unworthy. He just hoped he could make it up to her in some small way.

How he might do that, though, he didn't have a clue. Most of the night he'd lain awake thinking about them. He had never intended to cut off their relationship on leaving the island. It was just that he was preoccupied with Paula's message. Her call had awakened him from a blissful dream drenched in sunshine and loving embraces. She had forced him to remember the real world. The world of high-stakes business deals, seven-figure contracts and soaring revenues. He had to concentrate on his battle plans for winning back his clients, or his entire empire might come tumbling down.

But what about Abby? How did she fit into these plans?

Until a few hours ago, he hadn't known how to handle her as a lover, outside of their Bermuda paradise. But after a long night's thoughts, he felt he had a tentative grip on the touchy situation. He strode into headquarters with a renewed air of assurance.

Paula looked up from her desk in the reception area. "Good morning, Lord Smythe."

"Morning," he returned, driving toward his office with purpose. "Tell Abigail, when she gets in, I want to see her in my office."

"She's in, sir."

He stopped in his tracks, looked at his watch. "It's only eight-thirty."

"Yes, sir. She was here when I arrived, twenty minutes ago."

He hesitated. "How did she look?"

"Tanned," Paula answered dryly. She wasn't smiling. He suddenly felt in the dangerous position of being trapped between two angry women. But maybe not...

"Is she, um, ...in a good mood?" Her early appearance might mean that she'd forgiven him. That would make things so much easier.

"I'm in a *great* mood!" a chipper voice hit him from behind. "Why shouldn't I be? Twenty-one days on a tropical island, soaking up sunbeams, swimming with the fishies..."

Matt spun around to stare at a different Abby than the one he'd left in tears the night before. She had bravely pulled herself together and was putting on a great show of perkiness and goodwill. Either that, or she hadn't fallen for him as hard as he'd imagined. Was he that easy to forget?

She wore a smart forest-green suit that set off her red hair. Her eyes were bright and clear—their usual chocolate hue. She'd styled her hair differently, pulling it back from her face and up in a loose, tumbly sort of arrangement that did magical things to the long line of her neck. He could have devoured her on the spot.

All notions of business flew from his mind.

"Oh good. You're here." He coughed into his hand to clear the annoying roughness from his throat. "Can you spare a few minutes?" He held open his office door for her.

She breezed past him with a carefree, "Thank you," as if he were the doorman. He closed the door behind them and turned. She was already seated across from his desk, her notepad and pen in ready position.

"Abby, you don't have to—"

She looked up at him innocently, and all he could remember was that same look as he moved his body over hers the first time they'd made love.

"I'm sorry," he blurted out. "I never meant to hurt you or mislead you. And if you think I'm dumping you, that's not true."

"It's not? I certainly got that impression last night."

"I didn't have my head together, hadn't had time to work things out for us."

"For *us?*" Her tone caught him off guard. "But now you have? You have made decisions about our relationship...for both of us."

"Ye-e-es," he said slowly, watching her expression with caution.

She set her pad and pen on the chair beside her and looked up at him, her hands folded easily on her knee. "And?"

He sat on the corner of his desk and concentrated on the speech that had cost him a night's sleep. "I want us to stay together," he began.

She blinked up at him, but he couldn't tell if she was surprised or just didn't believe him. "Really."

"Yes, but not at work," he continued before she could voice the flood of questions he could see rising inside of her. "That wouldn't be comfortable for either of us. Before long, the whole company would have figured out that we were lovers."

"What about my job?" Abby rose up out of her seat, her eyes darkening to a shade he didn't remember. A dangerous hue. "You promised."

"I'm going to offer you something better." He smiled, imagining how pleased she would be once she understood. He reached for her hand and seized it before she could back away. "If you agree to resign from Smythe International, I'll set you up in your own shop here in Chicago. Your severance pay will cover the down payment, and I'll give you a zero-interest loan for the rest, with no obligation to pay it back if you can't. And so we can spend time together without worrying about who knows about us, I'll move you into a new condo a few blocks from here and cover the rent. What do you think?''

Abby gave him a long, cool look. "What do I think? I'm insulted."

"Abby—" Panic rushed through him. "You don't understand. I'm handing you your dream. The money to open your own business…a long-term relationship that I've never given another woman." He couldn't offer her more than that. And surely she shouldn't expect it.

She pulled her hand free of his. "What do you expect me to say, Matt? I want to be an independent woman with a husband and family in my future. You propose to keep me as your mistress."

He groaned. "It's not like that at all."

"It *is* like that, *exactly*," she said, pacing in front of him. "How can you be so self-centered? You want me handy for an intimate night, but not underfoot. You don't want your employees gossiping about their boss's affair with his hostess, even though that's the image you wanted to give your clients because it was convenient and helped your sales pitch."

"Abby, none of this is the point."

"What about your point that I was aiming low by limiting my goals to a little coffee shop in Chicago? What about my learning the business and thinking international?"

"You could still do that, if you wanted," he said quietly, feeling he'd somehow lost control of the negotiations.

"But you'd prefer I stay where you can find me and you want to continue sleeping with me with no strings attached." She glared at him in challenge. He'd never seen her so vibrant, so quick with thought and word. She made him furious. He wanted to argue with her some more. He felt hot and excited.

"What man wouldn't want to sleep with you?" He gave her a calculatedly wicked smile.

It didn't work. She chilled him with an icy glare, then her expression mysteriously shifted. "I received a phone call last night, from my former fiancé."

Matt frowned. "Oh?"

"He's been trying to get in touch with me and left messages on my machine while I was away. He wants to see me."

"And you will tell him you don't want to, of course."

She shook her head. "I haven't decided yet."

"What?" An emotion purely male, hostile, and possessive seized him by the throat. The muscles of his abdomen clenched at the image of Abby in the arms of another man. "If you're trying to make me jealous—"

"I know that wouldn't work, and I wouldn't stoop that low anyway," she said quickly. "But hearing from Richard made me think about why you and I first became intimate. I still want to be married some day, Matt. But that can't happen if I'm locked into a relationship with you."

With an intuitive flash he understood. Abby wasn't the sort of woman to emotionally or physically hold back part of herself for the next man to come along. If she was involved with him, she would stop looking for that husband of her girlhood dreams. They would stay together for a year…two…five…maybe longer. But when it ended she'd be right back where she'd started, without a husband—although she'd have a business of her own. Now he understood the fine line her heart had drawn. She would not surrender that part of her dream for him.

He heard himself give up a bitter laugh. "I thought *I* was the one who would have to pry myself loose from the naïve young woman."

"Life is full of surprises."

He shot a look at her, but there was no harshness or triumph in her expression. "Yes," he murmured. "Surprises." He took a deep breath. "If you won't accept the condo or the coffee shop, what will you do?"

"Work for Smythe International…if you'll allow me to stay."

He frowned. "Abby, do you really think that's wise? We'd see a lot of each other, and that's going to be painful for both of us."

"I enjoyed sleeping with you. But now that our affair is over, I can deal with it." Her voice was a mere whisper. It tantalized him, summoning memories almost too sweet to savor, now that he knew they would never be more than memories. "I love my job, the people who work with me, and all that I'm learning about this business. Why should I give up all these things just because we didn't work out."

*But we did work out!* he wanted to shout. *We were perfect together!*

However he couldn't say those words out loud. It was clear her view of a successful relationship was different from his. Marriage wasn't on his agenda.

"I'd value your help if you do stay," he said in a controlled voice, letting his eyes drift down her slim green suit then up again, recalling the soft curves underneath that produced that lovely silhouette. "You're sure about this?"

"I know what I want," she said confidently, her eyes sparkling in a way that all but did him in.

Abby walked out of Matt's office, chin raised, eyes dry, her self-esteem up two notches...even though her hands wouldn't stop trembling. Paula shot a quick look to see that her boss's door was closed. "How'd it go?" she whispered.

Abby shrugged. "He doesn't know what hit him."

Paula winked. "Go, girl. I told you—as long as you show no fear and stand by your guns, he can't bully or intimidate."

It wasn't the possibility of intimidation Abby feared. It was the danger of being seduced again by the steamy look in Matt's eyes when he wanted her. She hoped with all her heart that she would be strong enough to resist when they were forced to work late into the nights or traveled together.

Back in her own office, Abby punched in the number for her apartment. Dee answered on the second ring. "Yeah?"

"I survived, thanks to Paula's coaching." Abby collapsed in her desk chair and spun it around to gaze out on a gray Lake Michigan. It looked like rain.

"I'm guessing he didn't propose marriage when you told him he was no longer welcome in your bed?"

Abby laughed in spite of her aching heart. "No. He wanted to set me up in a shop of my own, a discreet distance away, and a condo close enough for drop-in visits."

"No kidding! So you said?"

Abby related the whole story, leaving out how her heart had beat against her ribs and her stomach had twisted into knots the entire time she was in the room with Matt. It finally struck her that the last time she'd made love with him really had been *the last time,* ever. She had made the rules. Now she would have to play by them. For if she gave in to his charm, even one more time, she knew she'd be no better off than any other woman the young earl of Brighton had dallied with.

On the other hand, what chance did she have of ever finding a man to live up to Matt? No lover would ever excite her the way he had. No man would ever bring her such joy, satisfaction or admiration. It had taken him only a few weeks to spoil her for all others.

Matt was aware only of the dying light through the sweep of glass along the south wall of his office. The skyline of Chicago faded quietly into a purple dusk. Lights came on across the city. The lake, so much a part of the spectacular view from his window, shifted from blue-gray to a somber charcoal, then to an invisible black as night fell.

He felt as if he too were fading. Leaving a very bright spot in his life and entering a darkness from which he might never find his way out. Abby had brought him unexpected joy, and sweetly beckoned from him new and exciting feelings. Feelings he didn't know how to deal with and, when it came right down to it, feared.

A knock on the door lifted him out of his bleak thoughts. "Yes?"

Paula let herself in. "I'm leaving now."

He had assumed she had already left. So preoccupied had he been with thoughts of Abby, the hours had slipped away. "Thank you for staying so long. I hadn't meant to—'' The words clogged up his throat. His thoughts grew fuzzy. ''Would you mind staying just another five minutes?''

Paula nodded and walked over to the desk. ''What's wrong, Matthew?''

He shook his head, stood up and went to the windows. Pressing his hand against the glass, he felt the lingering warmth from the sun that no longer shone in the black sky. ''I'm...I guess I'm...'' He wanted to say afraid, but men didn't admit to that. ''I'm worried.''

''About what?''

''Abby. No, not about Abby,'' he corrected, shaking his head. ''Apparently she can take care of herself. It's me I'm worried about.''

Paula gave him a knowing smile. ''She's different, isn't she?''

He nodded, unable to negotiate the curve in his thinking and drive toward the next coherent thought. ''Yes, different. And she makes me very happy.''

''I guessed that when you didn't come back from Bermuda on schedule.''

''I've traveled and slept with other women,'' he said with male defensiveness.

''You scheduled your vacations as if they were business trips. You never came back late.''

He sighed. ''True.'' His mind started working again, but nothing that came to him made any sense. ''The thing is, she has her standards, her goals, and she's very sure of them.''

''Just as she should be,'' Paula said emphatically.

He cast his assistant a dim glance. Whose side was she on anyway? ''And I have my rules. They don't mesh. I can't give her what she needs—a husband and a family. And she can't give me what I need."

"Another lover? Is that what you need?" Paula asked patiently.

"No, not just another lover. I need a partner. Someone who stands on level ground with me, a woman who can share my business and my bed and make me equally happy in both settings."

"A woman who loves you for who you are?" Paula asked.

"Of course, that goes without saying."

"And what about you, Matthew? Would you also love her?"

*Love.* As soon as she applied the word to his feelings, it chilled him. He couldn't answer her.

"Let me tell you something about yourself," Paula said, picking up the black onyx paperweight from his desk. "You are a man who thinks he has to be the master of every situation. If you are the boss, you don't have to be a friend or a husband, or more than a temporary player in a sexual adventure. You don't even have to be a son to your father."

He looked at her sharply, feeling trapped and enraged by her meddling. She'd set him up for a lecture that he didn't want to hear. But he couldn't help asking the leading question. "What does my father have to do with any of this?"

Paula rolled her eyes at him. "It's pretty easy to see the truth, if you pay attention to it. You left England when you were twenty-one and you haven't seen your father since. You push aside every opportunity for love and happiness because you're terrified the object of your love will do to you what your parents did to you long ago."

He let the anger slip away and thought about that. Could it be so? "But Abby and I...we were absolutely open with each other. We cared for each other. She's important to me. I showed her that."

"Did you?"

Well, he had wined and dined her at posh restaurants. He had taken her to romantic beaches. They had ridden in a carriage through the moonlight, and he'd asked her to stay with him and be his...*his what? His mistress?*

"Have you done anything to show her how deeply you feel about her, anything that you wouldn't have done with another woman?" she asked.

There was the offer of a continuing relationship, but anything more would mean telling her he loved her and wanted to marry her...and that was impossible.

"I just hoped she'd know she was special. Apparently that's not enough."

Paula touched the back of his hand. "To love someone doesn't mean you are guaranteed love in return."

"I know. It just feels a hell of a lot better if it works both ways," he said with a dry laugh.

"It's all about taking a chance. You take risks in business every day. Why not take the one risk that might change your whole life for the better, Matthew?"

He didn't hear her leave a moment later. He stood at the window, seeing only dots of white light across the city, outlining buildings, streets, the movement of cars in the streets below. He wished Abby were here to share the view with him. Maybe he'd tell her how he really didn't hate his mother...he only wished he knew why she'd gone away.

*To love someone doesn't mean you are guaranteed love in return.*

It was true...his love for his mother, and even for his father, was still buried within him somewhere. It had never died. He had denied that love all of his life, and he was no happier for having done so. Wouldn't he be a fool to deny himself the chance of, just once in his lifetime, being loved back?

Turning abruptly, Matt reached for the telephone. He hit the speed dial button he'd programmed with Abby's number. It rang three times, then she picked up, and the sound of her voice sent ripples of warmth through him.

"Hi," he said.

"Matt?"

"Yeah. I was just thinking, if you haven't already eaten, maybe we could use dinner to talk about... about the Johanson account."

There was the slightest hesitation before she answered. "It's after work hours. I have plans for tonight."

He gauged the level of tension in her voice. She wanted to see him as much as he wanted to see her, he was almost sure of it. "All right then, will you have dinner with me to talk about us?"

"The only *us* involves work, and I'm not working tonight."

"Abby! This is insane. I need to see you and—"

"Good night, Matt. See you tomorrow at the office." The line went dead.

He stared at the receiver in disbelief. No woman

had ever hung up on him! He hit redial. The phone rang six times, then was picked up.

"Don't do that again!" he growled.

"*I* didn't hang up on you the first time, but I will now if you don't stop harassing my roommate," a deep female voice threatened.

"Dee? Put Abby on the phone. I know she's still there."

"She doesn't want to speak to you or see you outside of the office," she stated coolly.

He groaned. What could he do but hope Abby would eventually come to her senses? However, to change her view of him, he'd have to talk to her...and he couldn't very well do that at work with other people around.

In the days that followed, he tried to find an opportunity to talk to Abby. But it seemed that she was never alone. If Paula wasn't with her, one of the sales reps was meeting with her, or she was dashing out the door on errands she insisted were necessary to one or another of his deals.

Five days later, on a Friday night, he ran out of patience. He decided he wouldn't call, he would go directly to her apartment. Together, they would figure out what was to become of them. He would ask her to move in with him. To hell with office gossip. He would still give her the option of her own shop, or let her stay on and work with him...but none of this cold shoulder business. They would be lovers and if anyone didn't accept that, it was just too bad. There was something liberating about living the way he wanted to, not caring what others thought.

Abby would have her job and a long-term relationship. It would have to be enough. If she wanted to have children…well, he'd see if he could even handle that. In the meantime, there should be at least some compromise. Right? He had to leave an escape hatch for himself. A back door, a tunnel to freedom if she lost interest in him or it turned out she had never really loved him. Above all, he wouldn't end up the one left behind. Not again.

# Ten

---

At the sound of the knock on her door, Abby straightened her dress, ran fingers through her hair, and checked her lipstick in the mirror. He had called, and she was expecting him. The conversation they would have wasn't one she was looking forward to, but it would have to happen. It helped to know she looked as good as she possibly could before facing him.

But when Abby opened the door, the person standing on the other side wasn't who she'd expected. She fell back a step in surprise. "Matt?"

"I hope you don't mind my dropping by without calling." He held out a bouquet of flowers to her. She stared numbly at them.

"I...well, they're lovely of course...but now isn't a good time."

"It's now or never," he said grimly, stepping into

her apartment. He crossed the living room and looked around, as if to find a handy vase. At last he laid the bouquet on the low, glass coffee table. "We need to talk. I believe we can come to a compromise on this issue."

"This *issue?*" She quirked a brow at him. "You and I aren't participants in a business merger. We're people, with feelings and needs and...and right now," she continued hastily, "I need you *to leave.*"

"No," he said and sat down on her couch.

Abby looked nervously at the clock on her wall. If she didn't get him out of here fast, all hell was going to break loose in a matter of minutes.

"I'm expecting someone," she said softly.

He stared up at her as if unable to translate her words from a foreign language. "I won't get in your way," he said. "I'll just wait until you're finished with—"

She was shaking her head. "He'll be here any minute, and we—he and I—need to be alone to talk."

She could see the reality of the moment sinking in, slowly, by increments. Matt's expression darkened. His hands, resting at his sides on her sofa, rolled into tight fists. When he spoke, his voice was low and tight. "You have a *date?*"

"Richard is coming over."

"Richard," he said dully. "Getting back with that loser isn't going to solve anything, Abby."

"What we do or do not do is none of your business," she said sharply. "Now I'm asking you to leave."

"No," he repeated with renewed emphasis. He sat deeper into the sofa cushions and gave her a stubborn smile.

Abby rolled her eyes toward the ceiling, now resigned to a confrontation between the two men who had had the most impact on her life. One she once had promised to marry; the other she had desperately wanted to marry.

Her mind whirled with options. She couldn't physically force Matt out of her apartment, and she wouldn't call the police on him. She glanced hastily again at the clock. She might try catching Richard on his cell phone and heading him off until she was able to convince Matt to leave.

The doorbell rang. Both Abby and Matt snapped around to stare at the door. Slowly, Matt leaned back in his seat, linking his wide fingers over one knee. He smiled in challenge at her. "Can't wait to meet your Richard. Aren't you going to let him in?"

She felt as if she were taking that last, long walk toward her own execution. Finding herself facing the door, hand on the knob, she stared down at her fingers as they shakily turned it. She looked up to see a stranger...maybe.

"Richard?"

"Like the beard?" He swooped down on her, looping an arm around her waist, hoisting her up to him and planting a sloppy kiss on her mouth. "Hey, you look gorgeous! Here, these are for you."

She looked to her right at a big bunch of daisies. Her favorite flower...at least they had been until she'd met Matt. Now she was partial to hibiscus. Island hibiscus in tropical shades.

"They're...they're very nice, Richard." She backed out of his embrace and chanced a quick glance at Matt. His face was stormy. He was glaring at the other man as if Richard were an oncoming train. Matt's gaze swerved to Abby for an instant.

She looked away, blushing. "Richard, this is my boss, Matthew Smythe."

His face lit with a smile. "Ah, so you're the one who stole my Abigail from me." He chuckled. "Heard all about you!"

"You have?" Matt asked warily.

"Yes, of course, or rather I've read about you. The American Earl the tabloids call you, right?" He crossed the room to Matt and elbowed him playfully in the ribs. "Anyone ever tell you we don't have an aristocracy in this country?"

Matt grimaced with thin tolerance.

Abby stepped between them. "Matt was just leaving. We had an issue to discuss, but it's been resolved."

"Great." Richard stuck out his hand. "Happy to meet you, Matt. Treat my little Abby good on the job, won't you?"

Abby was seething. *His little Abby,* indeed. But she didn't correct him in front of Matt. If Richard's ludicrous possessiveness got Matt out of her apartment without a knock-down brawl, so much the better.

Matt stared down at the other man's offered hand, then away without shaking it. "Are you sure you want to do this, Abby?" he asked.

"I'm not doing anything," she insisted. "I asked Richard over to talk, that's all."

Matt looked at her, his eyes roaming her features, settling on her eyes. "I'm sorry I can't give you everything you want. But I know for certain, *he* can't either." Spinning on his heel, Matt strode through the open door.

Abby stared after him until she felt a touch on her shoulder. "There's something more between you two than work, isn't there?"

She turned back to Richard, the man she had once thought she loved, and felt only sadness. "I'm very fond of Matt," she murmured.

Hurt shone in his pale eyes, and bitterness seeped into his voice. "You only *think* you like him because of his money."

"That's not so!" she gasped.

"I'd bet you it is. I'm just an ordinary guy, but the earl there is a millionaire, and you want the things he can give you."

"That's not true!" she cried.

Richard's lip lifted at one corner in a snarl. "You're using him, Abby. Admit it."

All the anger, frustration and confusion of the week before filled her up and overflowed. She wanted to scream at him that she had no interest in Matthew Smythe's wealth, that she loved him for the wonderful man he was. But in the wretchedness of the moment, she wavered, questioning herself.

"Maybe I have used him—" her voice dropped to a whisper—"in a way." Abby turned at the muffled sound of footsteps in the hall. They were retreating. Someone passing by on the way to the stairs, she thought vaguely. "I don't know anymore. He wanted to help me, and I let him."

She was speaking of their business arrangement, but it was also true of their far more intimate relationship. He had ushered her into womanhood in the gentlest, most marvelous of ways.

Abby glanced at Richard.

His face was swollen and crimson with rage. "You

slept with him," he accused. "We were engaged to be married and you wouldn't have sex with me, but you *slept* with your boss!"

"This is not something we're going to discuss, Richard," she said, her heart thudding in her chest. "You walked out on our wedding. That was your final statement to me, as far as I am concerned."

He was breathing hard, his eyes darting around the room as if searching for a reasonable motive for her behavior...or maybe for something to heave at her. "I wasn't rich," he bellowed, "so you saved yourself for someone who was! You...you little—"

"Get out!" Abby ordered. "Get out of my home." She stepped toward him, her chin up, eyes blazing, forcing him to back away. He was coming perilously close to calling her a name she could never forgive him for.

Without another word, he stormed out the door, slamming it behind him. Abby collapsed on her couch, buried her face in her arms and wept. It had all gone so wrong. Richard had called nearly every night, and she had wanted to have one final heart-to-heart with him, to calmly explain that, whatever they might have had together, was now over. Her life had changed. Her dreams had grown since he'd known her. She had made a mistake by ever promising herself to him. She would have told him, as graciously as possible, that he had done them both a favor by walking out on the marriage, for they had never been a good match.

But as soon as Matt had shown up, she lost control of the situation. Sobbing into her arms, she gave herself up to a disappointment so devastating she knew she would never be the same.

*  *  *

Matt walked all night long, remembering the last time he had done this, in Bermuda. By morning, he couldn't remember where he'd been or how the hours had passed. He recalled stopping in a good many bars, but hadn't drunk all that much. Just stayed long enough to rest and warm up from the chilly night. Then he was off again.

He ended up downtown, across from the Art Institute, in front of a boutique with a trendy window display. Shuddering, he brought back the dark thoughts that had haunted him during the bleakest hours of his life. Hours that matched in pain the loss of his mother, so very long ago.

Now he had lost Abby.

The worst part of it was, he had lost her without ever really possessing her. He had thought that she might have fallen in love with him, but he'd learned otherwise that night. Unable to leave her with Richard Wooten, he had lingered outside her door. Not to intentionally eavesdrop on their conversation. He had wanted to make sure she was all right. Then he had heard from her own lips that she had used him. She had been attracted to his money and all it might mean to her dreams. That had crushed him. He had looked into her soul and believed she was as innocent of deception and as loving as any woman he'd ever known. Apparently he had been wrong.

He didn't stop by his apartment, just kept on walking to his office. Paula looked up with a smile that immediately dimmed when she got a good look at him. He had forgotten he'd asked her to come in that Saturday.

"What happened to you?" Standing up from her

desk, she came around to meet him. "Matt, are you all right?"

"Fine," he mumbled, not breaking stride on his way past her into his office. He must look a grimy, rumpled sight. "I need coffee. And fruit if the deli downstairs is open."

He closed the door behind him, pulled a spare suit and fresh shirt from the built-in wardrobe at one end of the room, and quickly washed up and changed in his private bathroom. A few minutes later, he sat down at his desk to consider a future without Abby.

Exciting things were happening again for Smythe International. In the days since his return from Bermuda, he had saved two at-risk accounts and been given an opportunity to buy out one of his competitors. Six months ago, that prospect would have sent adrenaline racing through his body. Today, he couldn't give a damn.

Paula let herself into his office. He looked up at her hopelessly.

"Care to tell me what happened last night? Looks like you've been drug through the streets." She set a tray on the desk in front of him, poured hot coffee from a carafe. A bowl of fresh melon, mango and pineapple rested along with a muffin beside his cup.

"A disappointment," he said, not wanting to show how much he hurt, while perversely hoping Paula would pry details from him. He longed for someone to agree with him that life was unfair and he'd been cruelly shortchanged.

"Does this involve Abby?" Paula asked quietly.

He looked up at her through eyes that burned from too much cigarette smoke and too little sleep. "You're good at this."

"I know," she said a little smugly. "Two sons who've already had their share of woman trouble have trained me well. What did you do, Matthew?"

"What did *I* do?" He was astonished. "I didn't do a bloody thing! I thought Abby was…might have been—" He shook his head, unable to say the words.

"In love with you?"

"Well, all right, yes. I thought she was in love with me. In Bermuda, it certainly seemed so and when we came back to Chicago, it was clear she expected some kind of commitment from me. I did the best I could for her."

"You did your best?" Paula asked, her look doubtful as she pulled up a chair across the desk from him. "What does that mean, Matthew?"

"Damn it, I told her I couldn't work with her while she was my mistress, so I offered her a shop of her own and a luxury condo."

Paula tipped her head to one side as if giving this serious thought. "Amazing. And she didn't appreciate your gracious offer?"

"Blew me off. She's going back to her fiancé."

"Really."

He was loosening up now. He felt he could spill it all out—the frustrations, the confusion, the yearning to be with Abby in the same moment that he ached inside, knowing she'd used him. He told Paula everything.

After a few minutes, she said. "Abby called me this morning."

His eyes narrowed. "She did?"

Paula nodded. "That young man of hers? She had asked him to meet her so that she could make him understand that they wouldn't be getting back together. Ever.''

"She told you this?'' He wondered how much more Abby had confided in his executive assistant. "What else?''

Paula shook her head. "Abby has confided in me. It's not right that I spill it all out to you, Matt. She's a very special woman, and I like her a lot. I don't want to see her hurt anymore than I want to see you hurt.''

"What about her using me for my money?'' he demanded. "She admitted it.''

Paula laughed softly. "If you believe she ever deceived you or cared one bit about your millions, you just don't know her.''

Paula reached out and laid her hand over his on the desktop. He felt no comfort, only a vicious pinching sensation in his chest. Still, as he closed his eyes and accepted her sympathy, he understood all that was in Paula's touch. If he'd had a mother, she couldn't have done a better job in a crisis.

She sighed. "Abby's one fault is that she follows her heart. If you can't give her yours, Matt, walk away from her. It's the kindest thing you will ever do.''

In the days that followed, Abby was aware of Matt spending more than his usual time at the office. He cut business meetings down to the few that were crucial. He canceled a trip to the West Coast. It seemed that whenever she left her office to meet with one of the sales reps or someone in clerical, Matt showed up, too.

She felt him watching her, studying her during a

reception they gave for two new clients, all the while turning over secrets in his mind. She wished she knew what they were.

They were rarely alone in a room, but even so she felt the eternal tug of his soul against hers. For a few weeks, they had become one. He had claimed her as no man ever had, or ever could again.

At meetings when they sat at the round, walnut table in the conference room, they were usually across from each other, separated by half a dozen people. The powerful sensation of being drawn to him always came. It was all she could do to stop herself from throwing herself across the table at him.

At times he seemed to be intentionally trying to catch her eye. She would look up from notes or a report, and find his gaze fixed darkly on her. Was he demanding something of her? She couldn't imagine what it might be. Hadn't she given him everything she was capable of giving?

One day she entered his office, thinking he had left for the day. Footsteps sounded behind her, and she turned to find him shutting the door behind them, his gaze firmly fixed on her.

"I'm sorry," she murmured. "I just came in for the Brinkley file."

Matt nodded but said nothing. He walked slowly toward her, making her think of a large cat, stalking a rabbit, its muscles tensed to spring, ready to respond to any defensive maneuver.

"I'll go now," she said.

"Not yet."

She watched helplessly, unable to move, unable to utter a sound, as he came to within inches of her. She could feel the warmth of his body in the narrow space of air between them. She fully expected him to trap her in his arms and kiss her feverishly. Instead, he lifted one hand and gently touched the tip of her nose.

"Where are you?" he asked in a husky voice.

She frowned up at him. "I don't understand."

"Where is your heart now, Abby? With your Richard? With me? Or off in limbo somewhere?"

She gasped at the candor of his question. It took her a moment to gather her wits. "Richard has left. He won't be back," she answered guardedly.

"And what about the other two options?"

She drew a deep breath, but it failed to make her feel any stronger. "I honestly don't know. We clearly want different things from life. I could give up an awful lot for you, Matt. But not my children, not the hope of spending the rest of my life with one man."

Now he did kiss her. Lightly. Lingeringly. She felt her heart leap into her throat. Her knees trembled.

"Come back to me," he whispered. "Live with me. We'll work out the rest, somehow."

She looked up at him, amazed by what she was hearing. "You want me to move in with you?" Marriage was the missing word. Children apparently fell under the miscellaneous category of "the rest."

"I don't care about office gossip," he insisted. "I want you in my life." His hands were moving up and down her arms, sending chills through her body. His lips touched her temple, her mouth again, her throat. More than anything, she ached to lie with him on cool sheets and let him do all the marvelous things he'd done to her in Bermuda.

But they were in his office, it was daylight, and there was no guarantee of privacy.

"Matt," she whispered hoarsely.

"Say yes."

She gently pressed against his chest. "No. There are too many unknowns. I can't risk moving in with you, not knowing what will become of us."

Frowning down at her, he touched his lips to her cheek. "I know what will become of us. We will be ecstatically happy."

"That's hormones talking."

He shook his head. "Much more than that," he whispered. "Give us another chance. We'll talk and make love and somehow, it will all work out."

She was as tempted as she had ever been. But a little voice from somewhere in her past warned her to be careful. He was committing to far less than she needed. He was promising her a home with him and wonderful sex and companionship...but to nothing more. When it came down to it, his idea of a successful relationship might be a month or a year. Hers was an eternity. Marriage, though no guarantee, was a firm commitment that she could honor and believe in, if he did the same.

"No, Matt," Abby said. She touched his face when it contorted with pain. "Not because I don't love you. Don't ever think that. I just believe you won't be able to change. You've removed yourself from your father, from your entire family, really. You've put up an emotional barrier between yourself and everyone else in the world. A man like that can't be trusted."

"Give me a chance."

She smiled sadly. "I can't risk my future on a promise that isn't backed up by some kind of proof." Tears welled up in her eyes and coursed down her cheeks. "Oh, Matt, this is the hardest thing I've ever done." She wrenched herself out of his arms and backed quickly toward the door to the reception area. "You'll have my resignation tomorrow. I can't do this any longer."

Abby ran from his office, not daring to stay a moment longer. Words came too easily to men, it seemed. Richard had made promises too, then changed his mind. The pain of rejection had been nearly unbearable then. But as it turned out, she hadn't even loved the man. If she trusted Matt but he eventually left her, it would destroy her. There was only one way to avoid that. If she walked out of his life now, while she still possessed a few shreds of pride, she might still survive.

# Eleven

The days that passed were gray and without purpose, it seemed to the young earl. It didn't matter whether the sun shone or a typhoon struck. A colorless haze had closed around him. He went through the motions of running his business—flew out to L.A. and returned, made a hasty trip for two meetings in Manhattan, signed on a new client. There was no satisfaction and even less joy in the things he had once thought to be the center of his universe.

Even when the day's agenda was packed, Matt felt restless. In the company of others, he felt alone. Abby had left him, and he tried to honor her decision by leaving her alone. He didn't call, didn't visit her apartment. But every day he drove past the building where she lived, and he gazed longingly up at the window he knew to be hers, wondering if she was at home, or off on her own or with someone else.

A month passed, and he made good his promise. Her severance pay was generous and would cover the down payment on a small retail business in a respectable part of town. Along with the check that he had had hand-delivered by one of his people, he included the name of a real estate agent he'd often worked with, and a reliable loan officer who would make sure she received the additional money she needed to start up her business. She was already aware of the major suppliers she would need to buy from; that much she had learned by working at his side.

He felt her loss with heartbreaking bitterness some days, with a sense of oppressive sadness on others. He hadn't wept since the day his mother walked out of his nursery. He came damn close to it on many mornings when he woke alone in his bed. He found a stray red hair on the shoulder of one of his suits, and it nearly undid him.

As the days grew cooler and summer came to an end with the falling of the leaves from the hills surrounding Lake Michigan, his loss became no easier to bear. One day Matt walked into the office and stood over Paula's desk.

She looked up as if she already knew what he was about to say.

"I have to give it one more try," he said.

She nodded solemnly. "I wish I could say you have a chance. But Abby may have moved on with her life by now."

*"Moved on*...code words for, *found another man."*

"Possibly."

He tried to swallow over the sudden rough spot in

his throat, but couldn't. "Have you spoken with her since—'' He gestured toward the door.

"We talk now and then," Paula admitted.

"And?"

"I think she's been dating. But I don't know if anyone serious has come into her life."

He took a deep breath and let it out slowly. He knew Abby. She wasn't one to do anything foolish like take a random lover on the rebound. But he had awakened desires in her that she hadn't known before. There would be feminine hungers to be fed, eventually. And he wouldn't be there to satisfy them. The thought drove him nearly mad.

"What are you going to do?" Paula asked.

"I realize I can't just ask her to come back to the company, or to me," he said tightly.

"Right," she agreed.

"I must do something to prove to her that I've made peace with my past. Only then will she be able to believe I'm capable of truly loving her."

Paula frowned. "And how do you propose to do that?"

"I haven't worked it all out yet. But I know I'll need your help when the time comes. Here, grab your coat, I'll treat you to breakfast. We need to plan our strategy."

Paula lifted her leather jacket from the hook beside her desk, but reached for Matt's arm to stop him before he moved toward the door. "Owning her isn't what it's about," she murmured. "Abby's not just another company to acquire."

"I know," he said solemnly.

"Do you love her?"

He didn't miss a beat. "With all my soul."

\* \* \*

Abby laid down the loan contract, her eyes lingering on it as she stood up to reach for the ringing phone. Dee rushed into the kitchen. "Oh, you've got it."

Abby nodded. "Hello?" she said into the receiver.

"It's Paula, honey."

Abby grinned. "Hey, great to hear from you! How's the gang doing?" She always asked in that way. Impersonal, no names mentioned. Never, ever Matt's.

Paula had told her weeks ago that a new hostess had started working for them, and she seemed to be doing fine. Abby didn't want to think about another woman traveling with Matt, staying in the lovely New York penthouse, sleeping in the breezy Bermuda villa.

"We're all fine…just in a bit of a pinch right now."

"Oh?" Worry prickles danced along Abby's spine. Although she was no longer working for Matt's company, she would always feel a warm attachment to things important to him. "What's wrong?"

"Kerri, our new hostess, has to go home for a few weeks while her mom has surgery. Matt's had big plans for entertaining some very important people at the house in Bermuda. It means a lot to him. But he can't do it alone, and I can't rush off and leave two teenage boys on their own, even for a day."

Abby reacted instinctively to Paula's urgent tone. "Is there anything I can do?" Later, she would realize that all she'd intended was to offer to call around and see if she could find a reliable substitute for Kerri.

"There is," her friend said quickly. "You can step in and be our substitute hostess for a few days."

Abby drew a sharp breath. "I couldn't. I mean, I have a new job and all."

"But it will only be for a few days and you know the routine. I can place the orders from here. All you have to do is hop on a plane, supervise the staff as they set things up, show up in a pretty dress and smile at the guests."

"Sure but, Paula, I honestly don't think I could face Matt. Not there. That house holds too many memories."

"I know, dear," she said at last. "It's almost like someone dying, isn't it? You need closure. You need to face Matt one last time. Show him and yourself that you're going to be all right with or without him. Only then will you be at peace with your decision."

"I don't know…" Abby sighed.

"He needs you," Paula whispered. "More than you know. You may not believe this, but he's given you more than he's allowed any other woman. Do just this one small favor for him. For all of us. Please."

Abby closed her eyes. Her head throbbed and hands trembled. Was she really strong enough to do this? "I'll do it for *you*, Paula. I know what a bear he can be when things don't work out his way. He'll be impossible to work with."

Abby thought she heard a muffled yip of triumph from the other end of the line. "What?"

"Nothing, dear," Paula said. "I'm just so very relieved. Now let's talk details."

Three days later, Abby arrived at the airport near the St. George's end of the island. Matt's driver was waiting for her just beyond Customs.

"Hello, Ramon, it's good to see you again," she said as he took her overnight bag from her.

"My wife and I have missed you," he responded with genuine warmth. "Maria enjoyed having your company."

"And I enjoyed hers," Abby admitted, a twinge of regret cutting off further words. Better get straight to business. "Is there a lot to be done before the reception?"

He gave her an odd sideways look. "Not so much. Most of the guests arrived yesterday. The earl has taken them for a day-long fishing trip. They won't be back until this evening. Maria is not looking forward to that."

"Why is that?" she asked, smiling at the face he was making.

"All those smelly fish to clean."

Abby laughed. "Then we'll just have to lend a hand, won't we?"

The drive to Smythe's Roost, in the middle of the island, took less than thirty minutes, even during the busiest time of the day. Between noon and two in the afternoon, offices in Hamilton, the capitol, virtually emptied out as employees took their lunch breaks. Few seemed inclined to the American workaholic's practice of eating at one's desk.

The villa was as beautiful as she remembered it. Flowers bloomed in profusion in the gardens. The darling tree frogs whistled their love calls. Colorful birds flitted through the tops of soaring royal palms. Playful lizards darted behind thick foliage as the car passed. This was truly a tropical paradise.

In a second's flash, Abby remembered all the happy times she and Matt had shared, before she was overcome by a surge of regret. In two days, she would leave Bermuda, having seen Matt for what must surely be the very last time. She prayed Paula was right and this would be a final, cleansing experience for her—proof that she was indeed over him.

Maria greeted them in a vivid orange dress at the back door. "Come in, come in, missus. We are so excited to have you back."

"Thank you," Abby murmured graciously, although her heart ached and her stomach was cramping with nerves.

Ramon led the way up the curve of stairs to the second floor, carrying her luggage. When he reached for the door to the master bedroom, Abby held out a hand to stop him. "No. The earl and I...surely he told you that I was to have a separate room."

He smiled at her over his shoulder. "Lord Smythe said this one was for you. You would feel most comfortable here. He has taken another."

"Oh," she said feeling foolish for jumping to conclusions. Matt would no more want to put himself in such an awkward situation than she would. "Of course."

The room was even more lovely than she remembered it. Pale gauze curtains drifted inward on the breeze off Hamilton harbor. The scent of frangipani and honeysuckle came through the open windows. White wood furnishings were offset by cool, pastel splashes of pink and mint green on the bedding and in the watercolor prints on the walls. It was a room that soothed and welcomed, and lowered the blood pressure just by stepping into it.

Abby took only enough time to unpack her few toiletries and hang the dress she would wear that night. The remaining few items of casual clothing she had brought, she left in her travel bag. For such a short trip, it made no sense to transfer things into drawers.

After freshening up and applying a fresh coat of lipstick, she set out for Matt's study. As she'd expected, he had left instructions for her on his desk. She set to work organizing the lovely salon that opened onto a veranda at the back of the house. He wanted a champagne toast to start off the evening, along with simple canapés, imported caviar and a selection of tropical fruits and cheeses. She tried to choose items that complimented the French champagne, and wondered why he had chosen that beverage when he normally liked a variety of wines and cocktails to offer his guests. She decided this must indeed be a very special occasion for him, just as Paula had indicated.

By five o'clock she had finished and everything was ready for the guests. They had yet to appear, which was probably fortunate. She'd have time to change, then greet everyone as they arrived at the reception. She asked Maria for a guest list and the files Matt always kept on each client. The cook looked worried and avoided meeting Abby's questioning gaze.

"He left nothing like that," she said quickly. "Lord Smythe will be there to introduce you to everyone."

Abby shrugged. Whatever the man wanted…

She went off to change her clothes and do her hair. Champagne required a sophisticated French twist, she decided. With her hair pinned up, gold earrings in her lobes, and a beaded black cocktail dress she had bought in New York while she had still been working for Matt, she felt on top of her game. Nothing would rattle her tonight, she told herself—there were emotional hurdles but she would clear them.

To Abby's surprise, as she approached the salon, she heard voices. She walked in to find several couples chatting, clustered around an older man who seemed the focus of everyone's attention. She immediately sensed that everyone knew one another. More than that. There was a distinct atmosphere of conspiracy, as if they were all acting with a single purpose. One she didn't understand. Abby shot a hasty look around the room and found Matt, talking with a man and woman of unmatched beauty. She could only have described them as regal. The woman's eyes shifted across the room toward Abby; her smile was dazzling. She whispered something close to Matt's ear.

He turned.

Abby's heart simply stopped.

The expression in his eyes was impossible to turn away from. She tried to force herself to take a step forward, but found she could not. Neither could she back away from him.

In the next moment, he was striding across the room toward her, his hand reaching out, his eyes alive with anticipation. "Everyone, this is Abigail Benton. Abby once worked for me, but became far too important to my life to remain a mere employee."

She blushed and felt a rush of panic. "What are you *doing?*" she squealed under her breath. "I don't want strangers thinking—"

"They aren't strangers," he interrupted.

"Clients then. Paula said they were the most important people you dealt with."

"Important, but not part of my business," he said softly. "This is my family, Abby. They have come to meet you."

She swallowed, staring in horror around the room, finally beginning to recognize faces familiar from newspapers, TV broadcasts, gossip magazines. Her eyes flashed back to the couple he'd been talking to when she came in. "That's the king and queen of Elbia." She was shaking her head even while making a statement she knew was true.

"Yes, my brother Thomas and his wife are codirectors for their Royal Highnesses' personal charities. King Jacob will meet with the American President next week. We talked him into stopping off in Bermuda for a rest from his busy schedule."

"And...and the other two young men are your brothers?"

"Yes, that's Thomas and his wife, Diane, over by the canapés. Christopher is speaking with my father."

"Your father! But I thought—"

"We haven't seen each other in over a decade. I thought it was time."

She stepped back, shocked, wary, trying to remove her hand from his. But he tucked it firmly between his side and elbow, then led her farther into the room as the others watched with undisguised interest.

"Why?" she whispered. "Why now...and without warning me?"

"Now, because you told me once that life was too short and family too important to shut out. Why not tell you ahead of time? Because you wouldn't have come, and you had to be here."

"I don't understand." Her heart filled her throat. This was all too overwhelming.

"You are the guest of honor," he murmured with a devilish smile she found as disturbing as it was seductive. His lips brushed her ear, and she had to stop herself from jumping away from the heat in his touch.

Before she could object or ask anymore questions, Matt began the formal introductions. The wives of his two brothers she knew were both American women. She liked them both immediately. Diane was a down-to-earth brunette with four children, three by a previous marriage that, Abby gathered, hadn't been as happy as the relationship she now enjoyed with Thomas Smythe. Jennifer lived with Lord Christopher Smythe in a Scottish castle they were restoring. They were still newlyweds and had that honeymoon glow about them. The king and queen were dazzling. But Matt's father carried himself with stiff solemnity that bespoke a man of stature and importance. His sharp eyes never left Abby during the introductions.

"And now, the reason for our being here," Matt announced.

Abby turned back to face him with a frown. She felt at a disadvantage; everyone else in the room seemed aware of what was going on but she didn't have a clue.

Matt reached into the pocket of his dinner jacket and withdrew a small jeweler's box. Her first thought was that this was a belated parting gift from the company. But, if that was so, why was his family present? Then the truth struck her with an impact that wrenched the breath from her lungs.

"Oh no, Matt..." She tried to turn away, but he

seized her wrist and brought her back around to face him again.

"You have to let me do this," he said firmly. "Answer as you will, but let me say my piece." His eyes blazed darkly at her.

She stood, her body shaking, certain she would collapse on the floor in the middle of this distinguished assemblage. Closing her eyes, Abby wished for invisibility, a stock market crash, an earthquake... anything to stop Matt from saying the words she knew she could never believe to be true.

"Everyone in this room has been waiting for this moment for a very long time," he began. There was a low murmur of agreement. "For two reasons. The first is, I have held myself separate from this family for far too many years. I needed someone in my life to make me realize that one loss doesn't mean I should turn myself away from love forever." Abby stared at him. "The other reason is, they've wanted to see me settle down and do something with my life other than make more money...as lovely as it is."

There was gentle laughter now. But it stopped as soon as Matt opened the box in his hand and displayed a diamond the size of a large almond. Abby fell back two steps, but ran into Diane, who whispered in her ear, "Steady, girl."

She blinked at the stone as Matt slid the gold ring with the enormous solitaire onto the fourth finger of her left hand. "Oh...I don't know what to say!" Tears were flowing down her cheeks. This was all so confusing. It seemed such a cruel hoax. How could she ever believe that Matt meant to marry her when such a short time ago he had told her he could not?

With a heavy heart, she looked around at the smiling faces surrounding them. They were waiting for her answer. The world was closing in around her.

"I can't," Abby sobbed. Pulling off the ring, she pressed it into Matt's palm.

Abby ran for the veranda doors, pushed through to the garden and didn't stop running until she came to the far end of the flowerbeds. She collapsed onto a stone bench, buried her face in her hands and wept.

She wasn't sure how long she sat there before a deep voice spoke to her. "He's used to getting what he wants. Too much like his stubborn father." When she looked up, the old earl stood before her, his expression gentle and concerned.

"I'm sorry," Abby whispered. "I behaved badly in there. That wasn't a very gracious refusal."

"Do you mind my asking why you have turned down my son's proposal of marriage?" He waited but she could give him no answer. She couldn't trust her voice not to break. "To my knowledge," he continued, "no other woman has been worthy of his offer. Did you refuse him because you don't love him?"

She shook her head. "It's because I know, in his heart, he doesn't want to be married—to me or anyone else. I don't think he'll ever trust a woman to stay in his life. So he will eventually feel compelled to leave her…me."

"Because of his mother," the earl stated.

"Yes."

He walked around to her other side and sat on the bench beside her. "This is a good deal my fault. I turned my back on my family the day Anna left me. I gave up on my boys."

Abby turned to him, moved by the deep emotion

in his voice, something she was certain he rarely revealed to others.

"You loved her very much," she whispered. "What happened?"

"Anna was a free spirit, and I had a title, responsibilities, a serious nature. She stayed longer than I thought she would, giving me three sons. But when she did finally leave, after saying for years that she felt trapped, I was shocked. I didn't handle it well."

Abby was struck by a tenderness in his voice that seemed inconsistent with a man deserted by his wife. "You still love her," she whispered.

"Yes, although it took me a very long time to admit it." He gave her a sideways look. "I can only guess at the heartbreak my son has put you through, while trying to work out his own feelings. But I can tell you this. The four short years that I shared with that woman made everything else worthwhile. No one can guarantee love will last forever, but I believe that Matthew has come to believe, as his brothers recently have, that the risk is one worth taking. He loves you, Abigail. And you love him. What more can two people ask?"

There were tears in the old man's eyes when he finished. Swallowing over the lump in her throat, Abby blinked away her own tears. Then she leaned forward and pressed her lips to his whiskered cheek.

"Thank you," she murmured.

They sat in silence for a moment before she became aware of a shadow falling between the lights from the house and the garden bench. She looked up to find Matt watching them.

"You see how clever I am? Sending in the wiser, older man to soften you up?"

She laughed, her mouth still tasting salty. "You Smythe men are relentless."

"Aren't we though?"

"I'll excuse myself," the elder earl said, rising stiffly. "I believe the rest is up to you, my boy."

Before his father had disappeared through the hedges of roses, Matt knelt before Abby. She started to object, but only smiled at the old-fashioned gesture. "I don't know if you can trust me to give you what you need," he said, holding her hands tightly between his own. "But I swear I couldn't live without you now, Abby. You're in my soul. Marry me, please. You won't regret it, and neither will our children."

"Oh, Matt," she cried. "Is this real?"

"Absolutely real, my love."

Flinging her arms around his neck she squeezed hard as he stood, lifting her with him in strong arms. He kissed her soundly on the mouth. Their kiss deepened, and her heart soared. But she was the one to pull away.

"What's wrong now?" he asked, looking worried.

She beamed up at him. "Before I say yes, let me have another look at that outrageously immense ring."

"Yes, ma'am."

# Twelve

Abby's days took on a Bermuda-pink hue. She telephoned her new employer in Chicago and quit her job, then called Dee. Even after Matt's brothers, their wives and his father left for England, she drifted through rose-dawned mornings, sun-bright tropical afternoons and star-studded nights of bliss. Yet it still sometimes seemed too good to be true. And Matt must have understood her wariness for one evening as they dressed for dinner, he asked, "Are you still concerned about something?"

"No," she said brightly, then adjusted her answer. "Not concerned as much as puzzled."

He took her hand and they sat on the wide bed facing each other. "Tell me."

She struggled to find words that would make sense of her feelings. "It's just that you fought serious relationships and marriage for so very long. Then you seemed to so easily change your mind. I have trouble trusting sudden changes in people.''

He smiled down at her and combed his wide fingers through the screen of burnished hair that had fallen across her face as she gazed down at their linked hands. ''It wasn't as sudden as you might think, or as easy. But the battle has been won, believe me.''

She lifted her eyes to him. ''How do I know?''

He thought for a moment. ''Because it was such a difficult thing for me to do, taking that first step to reconcile with my father. For all my adult life I believed it would be impossible to approach him, to tell him how I felt—about my mother, about his rejection. Then I met you and I needed you in my life. And there seemed no other way to convince you I wanted to be part of a family, other than taking that dreaded first step to mend my past.''

''You did it for me?'' she whispered.

''Initially, yes. Later, after I'd spent several days in London with my father, I realized it wasn't all for you. I hadn't felt that good about myself in a very long time. I felt—'' he hesitated, searching for the words ''—whole again. Mended. Capable of being a strong partner in marriage, and a father.''

Tears threatened to fill her eyes, but she kept them back. Even happy tears had no place in this room with them.

''I am so very proud of you,'' she murmured and pulled him toward her for a sweet, sweet kiss.

The moment lingered.

And so did the kiss. It deepened and Abby felt a peace and trust that seemed as perfectly natural as the little frogs' concert outside her window. She let Matt pull her onto his lap and let out a soft gasp of surprise and pleasure as his lips trailed down her throat. She felt his fingers unbuttoning the front of her dress that she'd just finished buttoning. His hands moved inside her clothing. She pressed into them.

"I thought we had seven o'clock reservations?" she whispered.

"We do." He kissed the soft rise of her breast.

"We don't have much time."

"We have all the time in the world," he breathed, his eyes flashing darkly up at hers. The passion she beheld in his features left her weak inside, and summoned a familiar heat from low in her body.

"Perhaps, if we're just an hour late Maurice will hold our table." She arched her back as he leaned down and took her near nipple between his teeth and teased it.

"I expect it will be closer to two hours before we make it to the restaurant."

She smiled dizzily. Delighted. "Two hours?"

"Maybe more." His hands were very, very busy. And so was his clever mouth. Her body responded to him, as it always had and always would.

She leaned back against his strong, encircling arm and together they fell back against the bed. Reaching down, she freed him from his clothing and stroked the evidence of his arousal until he groaned deep in his throat. And when they were both wild with hunger for each other and neither could wait another second, she opened herself to receive him.

He filled her. Completed her. She gave herself up to him—heart, soul, and body—in the ecstasy of their embrace.

No longer did she doubt. No longer did she wonder at the miraculous changes she'd witnessed in this man. He was hers, she his. And the world with all its turmoil receded to a distant place that couldn't touch them as long as their love remained strong.

The castle rose above the village in Elbia, dwarfed only by the snow-covered mountains surrounding the ancient town. Locals called their royal family's residence, the Crystal Palace, for when the sun hit the rare white Russian marble, carved from quarries threaded with pearl-white quartz, its turrets glistened like cut glass. The day of Abby and Matt's January wedding, the sun's reflection off the sugar-white mountains and the castle walls was nearly blinding.

At first Abby had told Matt that she wanted only a simple family ceremony on her parents' farm. But as soon as she accepted the young earl's ring and proposal, the women of his family took charge of the arrangements.

"No, no," Jennifer insisted, "you must marry in London, in a beautiful old church. I can show you a dozen that would take your breath away."

Diane looked at King Jacob, as if they'd already discussed the matter. "There is another option."

The young monarch nodded at his best friend's wife then turned toward Abby and Matt. "My queen and I would be honored to offer the palace as a setting for your nuptials."

Abby gasped in surprise. "Oh, but we couldn't…" she shot Matt a look of mixed shock and delight, "…could we?"

"The decision is yours," he said with a smile.

"Well, I've always wanted to see Europe." She barely took a breath before making up her mind. "I'd love it." And so it was decided they would have as big and as formal a wedding as they liked, inviting all they knew to share their joy. After the ceremony, she and Matt would spend a month-long honeymoon touring the continent, from Paris to London, Madrid to Vienna. For Abby, it was more than a dream come true.

Dee was her choice for maid of honor and Paula, in addition to two of her best friends from college would be bridesmaids. The entire wedding party, including Abby's proud parents and Matt's family from England, were flown to Vienna and from there transported in small, joyful batches by royal helicopter to the landing pad at the far end of the palace gardens.

Abby wore a butter-soft, cream-colored velvet gown with fitted sleeves tapering to points at the back of her hands. The neck scooped low in front and rose in a high collar, elegantly framing her throat and face from behind her neck. Her soft red hair was piled high, and tiny pearls nestled in the center of each glistening curl. She felt like a fairy-tale princess, and Matt was no less than her Prince Charming.

In the days that followed the elaborate ceremony, the guests gradually left and life in the palace returned to normal. The King offered Matt the use of his jet to speed them between stops on their honeymoon.

"What do you think?" Matt asked Abby. "Do we zoom across Europe following each day's whim, or stick to our original plans?"

Abby thought for a moment. "I'd rather it be just the two of us, driving between cities, enjoying the countryside along the way. Would you mind terribly?"

"Not at all," he said. "That would be my choice." He kissed her on the lips and she looked up at him with love in her eyes. A love he feared he'd never quite deserve, yet would do all in his power to hold on to.

"Come on," he said, seizing her hand. His eyes were bright with boyish mischief. "I have something for you." He started up the wide sweep of stone stairs toward the private quarters on the upper floors.

Abby grinned and tugged on his hand. "If memory serves right, you gave me *something* already this morning…and last night as well." Would she ever get enough of his lovemaking, though? Perhaps not, but she didn't want to give his ego too much fuel.

"Not *that,*" he said, laughing, "although it's a tempting thought. This is a wedding present. I ordered it weeks ago, but it didn't arrive until today."

"I hardly need another present," she said softly.

"You'll like this one." He winked at her, and her heart skipped a beat.

They climbed the winding stone stairs, hand in hand, and she felt a bliss she'd never expected to know. Matt opened the heavy wooden door that led into their private chambers. The furnishings were massive, dark wood, centuries old, rich with history. On the bed, piled high with satin bolsters, was a tiny box wrapped in lavender paper. She sat down and picked it up.

"Open it," Matt said, watching her with delight and pride.

"All I wanted was you," she whispered. "We have truckloads of beautiful things to take home with us."

"Open it," he repeated firmly.

"Yes, Lord Smythe," she teased. Slowly, Abby pulled layers of paper from a white box, stamped with a distinctive gold emblem. Waterford.

"Crystal?" she asked. The box hardly filled the palm of her hand. "But it must be so small!"

"Something to add to your collection."

Grinning, she brushed her fingertips tenderly along the strong line of his jaw. She was touched that he had even noticed her inexpensive assemblage of glass creatures in her old apartment in Chicago. "How do you know it won't be similar to one I already have? Did you ask Dee for help?"

"I knew you didn't have this one. I commissioned the piece directly from one of the Waterford designers."

She stared at him in amazement. "You're kidding. It must have cost a fortune."

"Open the bloody box, woman."

She did, then lifted out a tiny, glittering figurine. Instead of being an animal, a fanciful unicorn or a butterfly, the delicate piece resting in her cupped hand was of two human figures. A mother and child locked in a loving embrace.

Tears filled her eyes. "It's the most beautiful thing I've ever seen," she whispered.

"I thought it appropriate, knowing your feelings about children. Besides, my love, *it's time.*"

"Time?" she asked, tipping her head to study his mystifying expression. He seemed serious, yet.... "You mean, *now?* You want to start a family so soon?"

He nodded, his eyes bright with anticipation.

"But you have a deal pending with that California vineyard, and there's the Russian caviar exporter."

Matt reached out for her and pulled her across the bed toward him. "Bermuda taught me one very important lesson. Work will always be there waiting for me. The people I love may not be. I want to fill up my life with you and our babies, Abby. There will never be a better time to start our family.'' He kissed her softly, lingeringly, then took the crystal figures from her and placed them gently on the table nearby.

''I've always said,'' she murmured, undoing the buttons of his shirt, one by one, as she pressed her cheek to his strong chest, ''there's no time like the present.''

''Agreed, Lady Smythe.'' He laid her back on the bed. And that afternoon, with a passion that would remain alive between them throughout their long marriage, they conceived their first child.

\*     \*     \*     \*     \*

**SILHOUETTE®**

*Desire®*

# Get ready to enter the exclusive, masculine world of the...

**TEXAS Cattleman's Club**

Silhouette Desire®'s powerful new miniseries features five wealthy Texas bachelors—all members of the state's most prestigious club—who set out on a mission to rescue a princess...and find true love!

**TEXAS MILLIONAIRE—August 1999**
by Dixie Browning (SD #1232)
**CINDERELLA'S TYCOON—September 1999**
by Caroline Cross (SD #1238)
**BILLIONAIRE BRIDEGROOM—October 1999**
by Peggy Moreland (SD #1244)
**SECRET AGENT DAD—November 1999**
by Metsy Hingle (SD #1250)
**LONE STAR PRINCE—December 1999**
by Cindy Gerard (SD #1256)

*Available at your favorite retail outlet.*

*Silhouette®*

#1 *New York Times* bestselling author

# NORA ROBERTS

brings you more of the loyal and loving,
tempestuous and tantalizing Stanislaski family.

*Coming in February 2001*

# The Stanislaski Sisters

## Natasha and Rachel

Though raised in the Old World traditions of their
family, fiery Natasha Stanislaski and cool, classy
Rachel Stanislaski are ready for a *new* world of love....

*And also available in February 2001 from
Silhouette Special Edition, the newest book in the
heartwarming Stanislaski saga*

# CONSIDERING KATE

Natasha and Spencer Kimball's daughter Kate turns her
back on old dreams and returns to her hometown, where
she finds the *man* of her dreams.

*Available at your favorite retail outlet.*

*Where love comes alive*™

Every mother wants to see her children marry
and have little ones of their own.

One mother decided to take matters into
her own hands....

Now three Texas-born brothers are about to discover
that mother knows best: A strong man *does* need a
good woman. And babies make a forever family!

*Matters of the Heart*

A Mother's Day collection of
three **brand-new** stories by

# Pamela Morsi
# Ann Major
# Annette Broadrick

Available in April at your favorite retail outlets,
only from Silhouette Books!

*Silhouette*®
*Where love comes alive*™

# where love comes alive—online...

## eHARLEQUIN.com

### your romantic
## books

- ♥ Shop online! Visit Shop eHarlequin and discover a wide selection of new releases and classic favorites at great discounted prices.

- ♥ Read our daily and weekly Internet exclusive serials, and participate in our interactive novel in the reading room.

- ♥ Ever dreamed of being a writer? Enter your chapter for a chance to become a featured author in our Writing Round Robin novel.

• • • • • •

### your romantic
## life

- ♥ Check out our feature articles on dating, flirting and other important romance topics and get your daily love dose with tips on how to keep the romance alive every day.

• • • • • • •

### your
## community

- ♥ Have a Heart-to-Heart with other members about the latest books and meet your favorite authors.

- ♥ Discuss your romantic dilemma in the Tales from the Heart message board.

### your romantic
## escapes

- ♥ Learn what the stars have in store for you with our daily Passionscopes and weekly Erotiscopes.

- ♥ Get the latest scoop on your favorite royals in Royal Romance.

SINTA1

If you enjoyed what you just read,
then we've got an offer you can't resist!

# Take 2 bestselling love stories FREE!

# Plus get a FREE surprise gift!

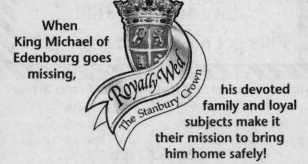

proudly presents the exciting miniseries

by bestselling author
# LEANNE BANKS

These super-wealthy bachelors form a secret
Millionaires' Club to make others' dreams
come true...and find the women of
*their* dreams in return!

**EXPECTING THE BOSS'S BABY—**
on sale December 2000

**MILLIONAIRE HUSBAND—**
on sale March 2001

**THE MILLIONAIRE'S SECRET WISH—**
on sale June 2001

*Available at your favorite retail outlet.*